A Small Boat

at the **Bottom**

of the **Sea**

A Small Boat
at the **Bottom**
of the **Sea**

~ john thomson ~

MILKWEED EDITIONS

Published 2005 by Milkweed Editions
Printed in the United States of America
Cover design by HartungKemp
Cover and interior illustrations by HartungKemp
Interior design by Rachel Holscher
The text of this book is set in Perpetua.
05 06 07 08 09   5 4 3 2 1
First Edition

Milkweed Editions, a nonprofit publisher, gratefully acknowledges support from Emilie and Henry Buchwald; Bush Foundation; Cargill Value Investment; Timothy and Tara Clark Family Charitable Fund; DeL Corazón Family Fund; Dougherty Family Foundation; Ecolab Foundation; Joe B. Foster Family Foundation; General Mills Foundation; Jerome Foundation; Kathleen Jones; Constance B. Kunin; D. K. Light; Chris and Ann Malecek; McKnight Foundation; a grant from the Minnesota State Arts Board, through an appropriation by the Minnesota State Legislature, a grant from the National Endowment for the Arts, and private funders; Sheila C. Morgan; Laura Jane Musser Fund; an award from the National Endowment for the Arts, which believes that a great nation deserves great art; Navarre Corporation; Kate and Stuart Nielsen; Outagamie Charitable Foundation; Qwest Foundation; Debbie Reynolds; St. Paul Travelers Foundation; Ellen and Sheldon Sturgis; Surdna Foundation; Target Foundation; Gertrude Sexton Thompson Charitable Trust (George R. A. Johnson, Trustee); James R. Thorpe Foundation; Toro Foundation; Weyerhaeuser Family Foundation; and Xcel Energy Foundation.

Library of Congress Cataloging-in-Publication Data

Thomson, John, 1954—
    A small boat at the bottom of the sea / John Thomson.— 1st ed.
        p. cm.
    Summary: Twelve-year-old Donovan's summer with his aunt and uncle on Puget Sound becomes a test of his own convictions when he suspects his uncle's involvement in a local racist group.
    ISBN-13: 978-1-57131-656-1 (pbk. : alk. paper)
    ISBN-13: 978-1-57131-657-8 (hardcover : alk. paper)
    ISBN-10: 1-57131-656-6 (pbk.)
    ISBN-10: 1-57131-657-4 (hardcover : alk. paper)
    [1. Uncles—Fiction. 2. Family—Fiction. 3. Self-confidence—Fiction. 4. Boats—Fiction.
5. Racism—Fiction. 6. Cancer—Fiction. 7. Puget Sound (Wash.)—Fiction.] I. Title.
    PZ7.T36954Sm 2005
    [Fic]—dc22
                                                                                    2004027250

This book is printed on acid-free paper.

MINNESOTA
STATE ARTS BOARD

in memory of

Rose Sovereign

restore, *vt*: to bring back to a former or normal condition, as by repairing, rebuilding, altering, etc. . . .

~ *Webster's New World Dictionary,* **Third College Edition**

A Small Boat
at the Bottom
of the Sea

~ part one ~

Thieves' Honor

~ one ~

No one uses this old boat dock anymore, no one except me and Uncle Bix. We tie our skiff to one of the pilings and think the high platform of rotten boards is good for some other things, like watching sunrises or measuring the depth of the tide.

"The wood is strong in places, but weak in others," Uncle Bix told me at the beginning of the summer. "A man just has to be careful where he steps," he likes to say.

The weak parts of the old dock are what draw me to it. Just one wrong move and you could plunge twenty feet into the cold waters of the Pacific Ocean. But if you make it to the last plank without falling, you feel big inside. You know you've chosen your steps wisely.

This summer, I've gotten to be an expert at reaching the edge of this rickety collection of pilings and planks. I've never fallen through—not once. When I get to the end, I like knowing I'm where no one, except Uncle Bix, can reach me.

Up to now, no one has even tried to trespass onto our private territory of wood, but today a stranger stands at the foot of the old dock. The trespasser is African American, and the biggest man I've ever seen. His legs remind me of the pilings holding up the dock's beams, and his shoulders are like a boat's stern, broad and straight, but able to roll with the waves.

He takes his first step and pauses when the dock sways under his weight. Then he looks at me in a bewildered sort of way, like a man who's suddenly forgotten his own name.

"You Bix Sanger's nephew?" he hollers.

"Yes," I reply.

The stranger stands still and spreads his arms to balance himself. He stares at his feet and soon walks with rhythm and confidence, as if he's just learned a new dance.

"Who are you?" I call.

He doesn't answer. His silence makes me wonder if he's a kidnapper, or a thief. I look down at the water and consider jumping. Then I turn to watch him. "What do you want?" I'm twelve. My voice is changing. It ripples through the air like a clarinet someone is just learning to play. When the stranger hears it, his mouth stretches into a weak smile. With this, I'm not so afraid of him.

He keeps on. His feet send tremors across the boards as he ponders his every step. He meets the challenge of the old dock and stands in front of me, with his hand out.

"Take it," he says.

I stare at his giant knuckles.

"Go ahead. Take it," he says.

I slip my fingers into his palm. He squeezes hard and my hand goes numb. "Your Uncle Bix is an honorable man," he says. "You always remember that. You hear me? You just always remember that."

He studies my eyes. He says the word *you* as if he expects me to perform some sort of miracle.

"All right," I say. "I will."

The stranger turns and looks back at the trail of boards. Feeling returns to my fingers. I'm certain he'll fall through this time, but he doesn't. He makes it to solid ground and then heads up the road. He's been on the old dock before, I think, or else he is someone used to walking on dangerous paths.

~ ~ ~

That word honorable would have been the last word I would have used to describe my Uncle Bix. Only one thing set him apart from other people, and it wasn't his honor.

He had this special talent for fixing things.

"Your uncle is a mechanical genius," my father once told me, during one of the few times he'd ever talked about his older brother. "He can repair anything," Dad had said. "Except his own life."

Uncle Bix's "own life" had been mostly a mystery to me. His very name was peculiar. *Bix.* How many people in this world are named *Bix*? In a way, it was perfect.

Bix rhymes with fix.

I'd asked my dad about my uncle's odd name as soon as I was old enough to consider such things. "He was named after a famous jazz musician who lived way before you were born," Dad had said. "Your grandfather loved jazz and thought this musician's name was catchy. That's it. It's that simple."

Somehow I knew it wasn't "that simple." Like most things with my uncle, it would just lead to more questions.

But I did know a little about him. I knew he was a lot older than my dad. I knew he'd always been kind of a hermit, and had "wild ideas." I knew he and my Aunt Hattie had been married for thirty or forty "rough" years and that they lived in a cabin on Puget Sound. And I knew Uncle Bix had served ten years at the state penitentiary in Steilacoom for being an accessory to a bank robbery.

I didn't know the particulars about the crime he'd committed, only that he'd handled the mechanical things having to do with the thievery, like disconnecting the alarms or jimmying the locks. While Uncle Bix was in prison, his misdeed wasn't talked about much in my family. I didn't know him well to begin with, and after he was "put away," as my mother called it, he became even more remote.

That's why the last thing I expected my parents to ask me to do was spend a summer with my notorious uncle. Why, if this man was so strange and corrupt, would they send me off to be with him?

Dad tried to explain.

"Your aunt and uncle need some . . . some, well, moral support," he said, stuttering a little. I'd never heard my dad stutter. Never.

"Having you with them will, well, lift their spirits, I think."

Dad teaches music at the junior high school I go to. Now, he was talking to me like I was one of his students who couldn't understand a complicated measure of notes.

"Look, Donovan, my brother needs somebody with him now," Dad went on. He pulled at his nose. His ears turned red. His eyes darted around as if he were following the flight of a moth slamming itself against a lighted window. "Your Aunt Hattie is sick," he said. "Real sick."

"Why don't you and Mom go?" I asked.

He wiggled his jaw muscles.

"It's not that we don't want to," he said. "But, you know, we think it would be good for you to go up. And, well, don't worry. Your Uncle Bix has paid his debt to society. You'll be all right."

We were on the front porch of our house in Portland when my dad spoke so awkwardly. We live in a cozy neighborhood in the old part of the city, near downtown. My dad's father, the same one who gave Uncle Bix his peculiar name, built our house. It's small, but big enough for the five of us: my parents, me, and my twin sisters, Holly and Heather. I call them "The Two H's." They're half my age.

They torture me.

"Besides," my dad continued. "This will give you a break from The Two H's," letting me know he understood I was at the end of my rope with my irritating siblings. He looked down at my feet and chuckled, no doubt remembering the time The Two H's painted my toes while I slept.

"So, what do you think?" he asked. I shrugged and chewed on my thumbnail. He was getting impatient with my silence. My mother was there, but up to now she hadn't said anything. Mom's a surgical nurse at the city hospital. She loomed above me as if I was one of her patients sprawled out on the operating table.

"You'll only be three or four hours away, son," she finally contributed, softly. "And I think it will be a growing experience for you," she said. "You can come right home if things don't work out."

I knew Mom and Dad weren't saying what really needed to be said. The truth was, they still couldn't bring themselves to lay eyes on my uncle, and yet they felt a family obligation to help him. They were going to use me as their emissary. Somehow they'd excused themselves from forgiving Uncle Bix by believing it would be a "growing experience" for me, and a chance to free myself from the torment of The Two H's.

I spared my parents the clumsy moment and told them I would go. I didn't like seeing them push a half-lie. And in a strange way, I wanted to do it. All those unanswered questions about my uncle faced me like the challenge I was soon to discover in the old dock. His life was like the mystery in the wood, strong in places, but weak in others.

~ two ~

My mother and father arranged for me to make the journey alone. "You're almost thirteen," Dad said. "You need to learn to get about in this world." It was another half-lie. The truth was they couldn't bring themselves to drive me to my aunt and uncle's hideaway. They couldn't let themselves get that close.

I took a bus to the nearest town, a place called Briar's Cove. Then I went by taxi down a curvy road to reach my aunt and uncle's cabin. They lived where the evergreen forest meets the sea. Coming down the hill to their place, I could see peninsulas and islands that looked like pieces of broken land separated by deep green ocean.

I saw fishing boats, some on the water, some hoisted for repair onto wooden racks. When I saw the beached boats, I remembered what my dad had told me on the way to the bus station. He said Uncle Bix made his living these days repairing the fishermen's vessels. His skill was legendary on Puget Sound. Fishermen relied on him because they knew he could fix something fast and right, especially when the salmon were running and the seiners couldn't afford to be dead in the water.

During the off-season, Uncle Bix worked on other things. Mostly, these were items people had thrown away, like sewing machines, toasters, outboard motors, tractors, lawn mowers, rototillers, weed whackers. You name it. When he decided to repair something, he wouldn't give up until it was back to being like new. Nothing seemed to matter more to him than bringing a broken thing back to life.

I learned this about my uncle the very night I arrived at his place. I saw him standing at the end of the old dock. My taxi driver honked his horn as the car's tires crackled over the driveway. Uncle Bix didn't pay any attention to the sounds announcing my arrival. He just stared out at the ocean, to a place not far from shore where the shadows of trees drew a dark curtain on the Sound. He fixed his eyes on the water just beyond the line of shadows, as if some magical thing beneath the surface was hypnotizing him.

The taxi drove off. I kept my eyes on my uncle until, finally, he jerked free of his trance and turned to approach me. He moved toward me over the rotten planks of the old dock without having to think about the dangers.

I'd forgotten what my uncle looked like. He was much shorter and stockier than I'd expected. He resembled my grandfather, and he looked nothing at all like my dad, who looked nothing at all like Grandpa. When Uncle Bix walked, he swung his arms back and forth like a gorilla. He was in overalls and tall rubber boots. He wore a baseball cap over very short gray hair. The rim of the cap was smudged with greasy fingerprints.

"You're Donovan?" he said.

"Yeah."

"Well, it's been a few years, hasn't it?"

I nodded.

"You remember me much?"

I shrugged. "A little," I said.

I heard a cough erupt inside the cabin.

"You know your Aunt Hattie isn't doing too well?" he asked. He jerked his eyes to the noise.

"Yeah. My mom and dad told me," I said.

"And they sent you here to give me a hand, I guess."

I shrugged.

"They just told me to help out wherever I can," I said.

He held his eyes on me for a moment.

"All right, then," he said. "Follow me."

He jutted out his chin and used it to wave me forward. He turned and walked back to the dock. When he got to the beginning of the wood, he said, "This old thing is real dangerous." And then he warned me about the strengths and weaknesses of the wood, and said a man needed to be careful where he planted his feet. "This time, you just step where I step. You got that?"

Just then I wondered why this man, who was supposed to be a mechanical genius, had left the dock in such disrepair. Were the Mister fix-it stories about him just that—stories?

"Okay," I said. "Step where you step. Got it."

He walked on, but took his time, always stopping to

see if I was following right behind him, stepping where he stepped. I could feel the wood move under our weight.

We made it to the end.

"You did good," he said. He stretched his mouth into a weak smile. Then he pointed to the place on the water he'd been staring at before. "There's a twenty-four footer resting off that little shelf out there," he said. "It's got a 315 horse-power Mercruiser 350 inboard in her. And I want it."

"A motor?" I asked.

He looked at me as if I were a bee that had just stung him. But my question was innocent. I really didn't know what he was talking about.

"That's right. A Mercruiser 350!" he said. His voice hardened. "And before the weather changes on us, . . ." He paused to inspect the sky, as if the forecast for the whole summer might be written on it. "We're going to pull up the boat, yank out that motor, fix it up, and put her into a classic '63 wooden Chris Craft."

"Are you allowed to do that?" I asked, respectfully. "I mean, doesn't it belong to somebody?"

"Look," he said. "There's a kind of unwritten law with people on this part of the Sound. If a man dumps his boat and leaves it for the crabs and mussels, then it's finders keepers."

He stared at me with a mischievous look on his face. He smiled and made his eyebrows bounce. And it suddenly occurred to me that my uncle hadn't asked me a single question since I'd arrived. No How was your trip? or Have you eaten? or How are your mother and father? Instead, he'd marched me to the edge of the dock and started talking to me in his foreign, boat-mechanic language. He had me look out at some invisible, broken thing that, together, we were going to bring back to life.

After we'd stared at the place on the water awhile, Uncle Bix had me follow him back. Once again he told me to step where he stepped. This time, I smiled when he said it. What if my father knew I was actually following in the footsteps of his wayward brother?

Maybe Dad never would have sent me here.

~ three ~

Aunt Hattie was in the kitchen, frying potatoes and sausage in a cast-iron skillet. She stabbed at the food as if it were a dying animal she was trying to put out of its misery.

An oxygen tank with a breathing mask was on the counter, resting in a place easy for my aunt to reach if she suddenly needed it.

"Well, look at this," she said when I came in. She ran her eyes up and down my body. "You've . . ." She coughed. ". . . you've shot up like a weed, haven't you? Just look at this boy, Bix. Look how he's grown up."

I was eight the last time I'd seen Aunt Hattie, when my mom and dad had let me go with her to Steilacoom to see Uncle Bix. She usually went alone, but that time, during another episode when my parents had me do their family duty for them, I'd gone with her.

I remember we had to take a prison boat over to the island. It was during a time when my aunt was trying to stop smoking cigarettes. She couldn't quit tobacco completely, though, and had resorted to smoking a pipe. On the prison boat that day, she'd gone on deck to light it. She smoked it as she stared out at the ocean and cried. I remember watching her. In her own special way, Aunt Hattie looked beautiful, even with the pipe between her lips and tears rolling down her cheeks. She had long black hair and a handsome, angular face.

She no longer looked like she did that day on the boat. Now she seemed smaller. Her shoulders slumped as if she might fall at any moment. Her black hair had turned a dull gray. Her skin was pale and full of wrinkles. Her voice had changed the most. It reminded me of a chain being dragged over rocks.

"Well, Bix!" she said, trying to act strong in front of me. "Did you hear me?"

"Yeah, yeah," Uncle Bix said. "I've seen him. And, yes, he's grown. More than I expected."

My uncle sat down at the kitchen table. He started thumbing through the newspaper. "But the hair's gotta go!" he added.

Uncle Bix no longer acted like he had just moments before when he'd led me to the end of the dock. Now he seemed grumpy and a little mean. I wondered if he couldn't be in a good mood unless he was talking about repairing something.

"Oh, his hair is all right," Aunt Hattie said.

"What do you mean by 'gotta go'?" I asked, softly.

"I mean it's too long," Uncle Bix spoke up. "If you stay in this house, young man, you wear a flattop."

I felt like saying something about fixing the sunken boat motor just to get Uncle Bix in better spirits.

"Oh stop it . . ." Aunt Hattie coughed and shuffled back to the skillet. She looked at the oxygen tank as if she was about to grab it, but she didn't. ". . . you just let him have the long hair if he wants," she said.

"Nope," Uncle Bix said. "It's coming off. You can fix it."

Aunt Hattie once had her own beauty shop in Seattle. She was a licensed beautician. No doubt she maintained Uncle Bix's flattop haircut for him.

"Let's not talk about this," she said. "Let's just eat, all right?"

"Fine," Uncle Bix said. He read the paper. "We need a hearty meal. We've got a big day tomorrow."

I sat next to my uncle. I looked at his hair. It was as short as a golf green and shaped like the bow of a battle ship.

"I suppose you're going to work on getting that boat up," Aunt Hattie said. She poked at the food one last time and then started heaping it onto a platter.

"Yep," Uncle Bix replied. "And we have no time to waste. We've got two or three months before the weather turns bad. Once the fall storms start to roll in, it'll be too late and—" He stopped. He looked at Aunt Hattie and then gave me a quick glance. "So, anyway, tomorrow we put a buoy on her," he said.

His voice softened.

"A buoy?" I asked.

"Yes, a buoy," he replied. "You're going to swim down and find her, then tie a buoy off on her."

"Swim down?"

"Yep. I've heard you're on some sort of swim team back home, that you've won all kinds of ribbons."

"Well, yeah, but are you saying that I'm going to go in

the water off that point out there and tie a rope to a sunken boat?"

"Yep, that's what I'm saying. Afraid?"

I didn't answer.

"Don't worry. It's safe," Uncle Bix said. "I wouldn't have you do anything dangerous. God knows your dad is mad enough at me as it is."

Aunt Hattie put the food down in front of us. It smelled rich and good. I was hungry.

"That's just terrible about that awful car accident in Seattle, isn't it?" she said, directing her eyes to the article in the paper Uncle Bix was reading. She was trying to change the subject. But, after learning what I'd be doing tomorrow, the last thing I wanted to hear was something about people dying in an accident.

"Dumb people do dumb things," Uncle Bix said. His voice turned mean again. "Besides, the fewer of those folks around here, the better," he added.

"Those folks?" I said. I looked at the newspaper. All I could see was a photo of a mangled car and glass scattered all over a highway.

"Never mind," said Aunt Hattie. Her face tightened. Beads of sweat appeared on her nose. I searched the newspaper for something more about the story. Uncle Bix quickly folded it up as if he didn't want me to see it. "Let's eat," he growled.

Just then Aunt Hattie started coughing violently. She put both hands over her face, hunched over, and stumbled to get her oxygen tank. Uncle Bix got up to help her. I looked at my food and found peace in the warmth and smell of it. My uncle got to the oxygen tank before Hattie reached it. He put the mask over her mouth as he embraced her. "There you go, Babe. Breathe deeply, now," he said. His voice was soft and kind.

She looked at him and tears welled up in her eyes. "You go ahead and eat," my uncle said, looking down at me as he led Aunt Hattie out of the kitchen. "Your aunt needs to lie down for a bit."

I was alone at the table. Seeing my aunt suffer like that made me feel empty and scared. I tried to eat, but my food now seemed tasteless and heavy. I could hear my uncle's voice in the back room. The hollow sounding words came through the walls. "You just let us make our own meals from now on," he said. "You're pushing yourself too hard, Babe. Do you hear me?"

I opened the newspaper to the article about the car accident. "Woman Killed in Interstate Collision," the headline said. There was a picture of the victim—a young African American woman. She was smiling, and very pretty. She was "those folks."

I heard my uncle coming back to the kitchen. I closed the paper and stared at my plate of food.

"Is Aunt Hattie all right?" I asked.

He sat across from me.

"For now. She's seeing her doctor tomorrow afternoon. That's why we're getting an early start on the boat."

"All right," I said.

We didn't speak again until after dinner, when Uncle Bix showed me where I'd sleep. It was a closet-size room with nothing more than a bed in it, like the berth in a ship or train. "We're up at five," he said. "So you'll want to climb in before too long."

I did. I went to bed earlier than ever before. I liked my sleeping quarters. I felt like an animal hidden safe and deep in a dry burrow during a storm.

I lay still in bed. Uncle Bix and Hattie's room was just next to mine, and their muffled voices came through the wall. At first, they spoke as if nobody else was in the cabin with them. Aunt Hattie, between coughs, strained as she mildly scolded Uncle Bix. "Don't you dare get that boy hurt out there," she said. "Things are bad enough between you and your brother. If Donovan is injured helping you pull up that boat, things may never get right between you two."

I didn't hear Uncle Bix's reply. Just after Hattie spoke, my aunt and uncle must have realized I might be listening, and the cabin became quiet.

I couldn't sleep. I was restless, and worried. Big questions I couldn't answer kept me awake. Was I going to lose my hair to a flattop? Would I be able to swim down and tie a buoy to the sunken boat, or would I hurt myself and completely wreck things between my dad and Uncle Bix? And, most of all, why had my uncle said those cruel things about the African American woman who'd been killed in the car accident?

~ four ~

It was still dark when Uncle Bix scrubbed my head with his knuckles to wake me. His rough hands scratching against my scalp became part of the dream I was having. It was a nightmare, really. Someone was giving me a flattop.

"Rise and shine," my uncle growled. I sat up and clawed through my hair. It was still there. All of it.

"You've got fifteen minutes," he barked. He left me and went to the kitchen. I smelled coffee and bacon. I heard Aunt Hattie coughing in the bedroom. I listened to it until it drifted off like a bank of thunder.

We did everything fast. We ate fast, dressed fast, and almost ran out the door. Just outside, Uncle Bix said, "This afternoon you can start splitting that wood over there." He directed my eyes to a pile of pine rounds. "Your Aunt Hattie and I will be gone a couple hours. It'll give you something to do."

It was a small mountain of wood. A maul was propped

against it. The thing seemed alive, like a person leaning against a wall, challenging me to a fight.

We walked to the edge of the dock and stopped. "All right," Uncle Bix said. "I want you to watch my steps again. This time I'm going to go a little faster. Can you do that?"

"Yeah."

Navigating the old dock was a little easier now, even though we walked more quickly than before. This time we didn't go all the way to the end. We stopped about halfway, where a skiff was tied to one of the pilings.

I hadn't noticed the skiff before. It was loaded with gear, lots of rope, a wet suit, fins, a diving mask with snorkel, and a big red buoy. The skiff was powered by some sort of antique outboard motor, but it looked brand new.

Another of Uncle Bix's magical repair jobs, I surmised.

He reached into the boat and threw out the wet suit. "That's for you," he said. "This water's fifty-five degrees. You've got to wear that suit or you'll cramp up."

"It might be a little small," I said.

"Well, you've grown a lot since I last saw you."

I picked up the suit and thought for a moment about what he'd just said. The last time we'd seen each other was four years ago, when I was eight, on that day I went with Aunt Hattie to see him in Steilacoom, the day she smoked the pipe.

"Can't you just *squeeze* into it?" my uncle pleaded, bringing my mind back to the present.

"I'm not sure," I said.

I'm very big for my age. And, yes, I'm an expert swimmer and have the broad shoulders to show for it. The suit was too small, but it was possible I'd be able to squeeze into it.

"Well, I'll give it a try," I said. "But what if I can't?"

"Think positive," he said.

I got the wet suit on, but it was very tight. I could hardly breathe.

"See, you did it," Uncle Bix said.

"Yeah, I guess," I replied. "But I'm not sure this is all that safe. I mean, it's kind of hard for me to take deep breaths."

He smiled and chuckled, the first time I'd seen him show any sign of being happy.

"Like I said, think positive," he repeated.

"All right," I said. "I'll try."

"Get in."

I climbed aboard and we headed out, pushing through a slight swell on the water. The sun was just coming up. It was a cool morning. Mist struck my face. I liked the feel of it.

The light broadened over the bay. Little cottages lined the water. They were tucked into the forest and connected by a road and a boardwalk. Smoke rose from some of the chimneys.

Uncle Bix stopped the skiff in the middle of the bay. We were still a long way from the point where I'd be diving to look for the boat. My uncle looked back at the cabin, turning an ear toward it. He's listening for Aunt Hattie's coughing, I thought, but all we could hear was the sound of water lapping against our skiff, and the cry of seagulls flying above us, watching, laughing.

"You know," he said. He looked at me. "Your aunt is pretty darn sick. Your father told you that, I guess."

"Yeah."

"It's lung cancer," he said. "Don't you ever light up a cigarette. You hear me?"

"All right," I said. "I won't."

He took a deep breath.

"So, how's your dad?" he asked.

"Fine."

"And your mom?"

"Fine."

"Your dad still teaching music?"

"Yep."

Uncle Bix looked off.

"Same school?" he asked.

"Yeah."

"Your mom still a nurse at the hospital?"

"Right."

"Seems funny I should have to ask all these questions about my own brother's family, doesn't it?"

"Yeah, sort of."

"You know the reason?"

I nodded, and then looked up at the seagulls flying overhead.

"Look," Uncle Bix said. "I'm going to tell you something, all right?"

"Sure."

I had a hard time looking into his face. I forced myself. His features softened in the dull light of the morning sun reflecting off the water.

"I've made mistakes in my life. You know that, right?" he said.

"Yeah."

"You can't go back and do something over. You can't

undo things. You can't rewind the tape and re-record. What I did was stupid and wrong, but . . ."

My uncle sighed again. He wanted to tell me something, but it was going to be hard for him.

"But," Uncle Bix said. He tried to lift his voice. "I wasn't a snitch. That's why I served so much time at Steilacoom, because I wasn't a snitch."

"You mean you didn't tell on the other guys?"

"Right. I didn't tell on the other guys. I wasn't a snitch."

We drifted in silence on the water awhile. My uncle wanted me to spend some time thinking about what he'd just told me, how a person can still keep his integrity even while he's committing a crime. I couldn't understand it. I tried, but I couldn't.

"It's absolutely perfect," Uncle Bix said finally, running his gaze along the shore with all the exposed drift logs and the flocks of sandpipers. It was as if the ocean had been rolled back for us. "I've been waiting a long time for a low tide like this," he said.

We anchored just off the point. The small wet suit was becoming more uncomfortable. I could take only shallow breaths. I felt like I was buried in mud from the neck down.

The water below looked deep, even at such a low tide. I stared at it. It stared back, daring me.

"It's only ten to twelve feet to the bottom," Uncle Bix said, noticing the worried look on my face. "And the boat's right below us. Get those fins and that mask on."

His tone was stiff and bossy.

"So," I said, pulling on the fins. Like the wet suit, they

were too small. "The deal is, I'm supposed to find the boat and tie the buoy to it, right?"

"Right. Just swim around down there first until you find it. Then come back up, get the buoy, and secure it to the boat."

"How do you know it's there?" I said.

"Know what's there?"

"The boat."

Uncle Bix looked at me like a parakeet staring at itself in a mirror.

"Oh, it's there," he said.

"But how do you know?"

My question felt bold, but for some reason, just then, my uncle seemed like someone my own age.

"Because Gus Hanks told me the story!" he said. "And I have no reason to doubt his word."

"What story?"

He sighed and looked away. My questions irritated him. I wondered why Uncle Bix didn't want to share the story with me, and I remembered something my dad once said: "If a man's got a clear conscience, and he really believes his own words, he won't hesitate to share them." Uncle Bix looked at me as if he'd just heard my father's lesson himself and suddenly realized the weight of those words was resting between us.

"All right," he said, finally giving in. "I'll give you the abbreviated version. The boat belonged to some rich and crazy computer genius who lived in Seattle. One night this so-called genius got drunk and took his boat out for a joyride. Rammed it right into that jetty over there."

Uncle Bix pointed to a small archipelago of rocks just beyond the bay. The rocks rose out of the water like the jagged spine of a sea monster.

"Then what?" I said. Uncle Bix groaned and rubbed his eyes. He was becoming annoyed, but I wanted to hear the tale.

"Well, this genius swam to shore and the boat drifted until it went down right here. End of story."

"And who told you this?"

He grunted tiredly.

"Gus Hanks."

"Who's he?"

Another grunt.

"Gus Hanks is Gus Hanks."

"I don't understand that."

"You don't have to understand it, Donovan. All you have to do is find the boat and tie that buoy to it. We need to take advantage of this low tide. Tides like this are rare."

"How come?"

"Do I look like an oceanographer to you?"

"Sorry."

I was ready. I swung my legs over the rail of the skiff and adjusted my mask and snorkel. The wet suit pressed against my chest, but I managed to take a deep breath. I turned to Uncle Bix to ask one more question. I couldn't help it.

"How come we don't just use some sonar equipment or something like that to find the boat?"

"Because, for one thing, I can't afford it," Uncle Bix said. "And for another, I don't think that sonar stuff really works."

"It works," I said. "I mean, I think it does."

"Are you going into the water or not?"

"Yeah, right. Sorry. But what happens after we put the buoy on this boat, if it's really down there, I mean what—?"

"We put a cable on her and use a winch to drag her out. I've got the winch already lined up. It belongs to Gus Hanks. He said if I located the boat I could use his winch to haul her up."

"But, what if—?"

"Just go!" Uncle Bix shouted.

I flopped in.

The water was very cold, but it was clearer than I'd expected. I dove straight down. I could hold my breath for almost two minutes, longer than most people. Still, I didn't want to go so deep I wouldn't have enough air to make it back to the surface. I immediately searched the bottom for the boat. I saw it. Gus Hanks's story was true.

The boat looked to be in pretty good condition, even though some of it was covered in green slime. I could see the name on the bow—Prometheus.

The water pressure at that depth made the wet suit tighten fiercely around my torso. I stopped my descent. I knew then that I wouldn't be able to get to the boat to secure the buoy line to it. Maybe, just maybe, I could do it if I had a wet suit that fit right and I had a few chances at it. I rose to the surface.

"Well, did you see it?" Uncle Bix yelled.

His eyes were like two full moons next to each other on the horizon.

"Yeah. I saw it."

"See. I told you."

"But I'm not sure I can reach it."

"What do you mean?"

I swam over to the skiff and used my arms to hang on to the rail.

"I think it's too deep. I'm not sure I can hold my breath long enough. Not wearing this wet suit, anyway."

His face sagged. He looked like somebody had just told him he'd shrunk five inches since they saw him last.

"But you saw it, right?"

"Yeah."

"How'd it look—I mean, what kind of shape is it in?"

"Well, I don't know all that much about boats, but pretty good, I think."

"So why don't you try again?"

"I don't think I can do it."

"Don't tell me that. I thought you were a champion swimmer."

"I'm on a city-league swim team. I'm not an Olympic gold medalist. And this wet suit is way too small."

I didn't feel that bad about arguing with Uncle Bix. He seemed to want me to tell him the truth about things, even if it meant sounding a little sassy.

"Could you do it if the wet suit fit properly?" he said.

"Maybe."

"Maybe?"

"Well, probably."

"Why don't you try just one more time? God, we just have to take advantage of this low tide."

I sighed.

"Just once more," he pleaded.

He looked into my eyes. Getting this boat meant as much to him as anything in his life, even Aunt Hattie. I couldn't refuse.

"Okay," I said. "Throw me the line."

"That a boy."

I dove again. This time I had to rise to the surface just after the boat came into view. I shouldn't have made the second try. I was less confident now of ever reaching the sunken vessel. Worse yet, I knew I'd have to do it twice, once to tie off the buoy and another to secure it to the winch cable.

"Well?" Uncle Bix said as soon as I broke the surface. He saw the end of the rope. "No luck?" he asked.

"Nope. Sorry."

"Stop saying you're sorry. You tried. Hop back in here."

We left the waters off the point and returned our skiff to the dock. My uncle had said nothing as we traveled across the bay. Sometimes he looked back to the horizon, perhaps disappointed that we'd squandered the low tide. But most of the time he kept his head cocked to one side, directing his ear, as if it were a radar dish, at the cabin. I was wrong about him and the boat. It didn't mean more than anything to him. Aunt Hattie was the most important thing in his life. I could tell by the way he listened for her cough.

~ five ~

"What's a Prometheus?"

I asked my question just a couple hours after my first dive. It was late morning, and Aunt Hattie and I were sitting on the porch. She was in a rocking chair, but she wasn't rocking. She'd been staring out at the bay. My question stirred her a little.

"Prometheus is a figure in Greek mythology," she said.

She seemed stronger today. She'd left her oxygen tank inside. She'd made a big pitcher of iced tea, and we'd gone to the porch to drink it. We used pickling jars as glasses.

"Prometheus stole fire from the gods and gave the fire to the people," she said. "And for that, the gods punished him."

"How?"

"They chained him to a rock. Each day, an eagle swooped down and tore out his liver, which grew back every night."

"How do you know all this?" I asked.

"I learned it in school back in Ohio. You should be learning it, too. Schools these days! They're shameful, just shameful."

She stopped to turn her attention to Uncle Bix's shop and the raspy sound of a power tool coming from it. He'd gone out there to piece together the winch cable we were going to use to pull up the boat. "Why did you ask about Prometheus?" she said.

"It's the name of the boat we're trying to get. I saw the name on the bow when I swam down to it."

She sighed and looked out at the water just beyond the point with the evergreen trees. "You be careful out there," she said.

"Do you think it's dangerous?"

I could tell she didn't want to answer this question. I thought of her warning Uncle Bix about my getting hurt, and how it would finish things for good between him and my dad. She looked away, closed her fist over her mouth, and coughed.

"Uncle Bix really loves fixing stuff, doesn't he?" I said.

"Indeed he does," she replied.

"How come he hasn't fixed the old dock?" I asked.

She smiled at my words, as if I'd just figured out a riddle. "He will, someday," she said. "I've learned, over the years, that Bix thinks some things serve a better purpose when they're broken. Then, when that purpose has been served, he fixes what was broken."

"So, what's the purpose?" I said.

"The dock forces him to be careful. And now it's forcing *you* to be careful."

"But—"

"Drink your tea," she said.

I took a gulp.

"Who's Gus Hanks?" I asked. She didn't want to answer that question either. But she answered it anyway.

"Your uncle met him when they were at Steilacoom together. He lives up the road a piece," she said. "And you'll have to excuse me if I'm not eager to talk about Gus Hanks much. I have a rather low opinion of him."

"Why?"

"Because he's a stupid fool, and he has too much influence on Bix—but don't you dare tell your uncle I said that."

"I won't."

"He'll be here in a few minutes, you know."

"Gus Hanks?"

"Yep."

"Why?"

"He's taking me and Bix to the doctor. Ever since your Uncle Bix got out of Steilacoom, he's refused to get a driver's license, and God help us if I were to get behind the wheel. So Gus drives us around. He does these little acts of charity to keep his hold on your uncle."

"What hold?" I asked.

Aunt Hattie didn't answer. Just then, Uncle Bix came out of his shop, dragging the cable behind him. It looked like a long metal tail. He dropped it to the ground and came to the porch. "Gus will be here in about ten minutes. Are you ready?" he said. He looked at Aunt Hattie.

"I'm ready," she answered.

"Remember what I said about that wood pile," he said to me. "Why don't you go ahead and get started."

He wanted to be sure I was busy doing something when Gus Hanks arrived. My uncle, it seemed, expected me to steer clear of the man. I couldn't help but wonder why Uncle Bix would have a friend he didn't want me to go near.

I went to the wood pile and picked up the maul. Uncle Bix watched me, and yelled out, "You're gonna need to use wedges on those rounds. There's some on the ground just next to you there."

"Right," I yelled back.

I rolled a pine round into place and drove in the first wedge. The wood was green and full of knots. The wedge barely penetrated it. As I reached for another wedge I heard a car approaching on the gravel road. Then I saw it. It was one of those big older models, a Lincoln Continental, with whitewall tires. Two people were in it.

I returned my attention to the wood. I tapped the second wedge into it and swung my maul, but missed. The wedge flew out and landed on my big toe. It didn't hurt. Much.

I looked back at the big car and watched the two people get out. One was a man about Uncle Bix's age, maybe a few years younger. The other was a kid, about my age, maybe a little older. It was hard to tell.

The man had to be Gus Hanks. This was confirmed when I heard my uncle yell out, "Hey, Gus, thanks for coming. We'll be with you in a minute."

Gus Hanks was a compressed man with a barrel chest, broad thighs, and an unusually large head. Like my uncle, he wore a flattop haircut. His hair was the color of rusted metal. He wore jeans and a long-sleeved white shirt with red suspenders. "No problem," he answered. His voice was like the meow of a hungry cat.

The kid with him was thin and had a very long neck

with a prominent Adam's apple. His neck reminded me of a limb broken from the trunk of a straight tree. He was a lot smaller than Gus. He wore no shirt and had a couple of tattoos on both arms. His head was shaved. He'd probably have a goatee on his chin, I thought, if he were old enough to grow one.

I took my eyes off the two of them when the kid noticed me staring. He came around the car and approached me.

"Earl! Where you going, boy?" Gus said.

Earl didn't pay any attention to Gus, who, I guessed now, was Earl's father. As Earl came closer, I saw the family resemblance.

I was rearing back to strike another blow on the wedge when Earl spoke. "What are you doing, dude? Haven't you ever chopped wood before?"

"Yeah, I've chopped wood before," I said.

"Don't be a wise guy," he said. He glared at me as if he were about to pull my ears off. "Give me that thing, you wimp."

"Earl, get over here!" Gus shouted. Once again Earl ignored his father. By now, my aunt and uncle had come out of the cabin. When they saw Earl standing next to me they looked at me as if I was about to step into a wall of flames. "You leave him alone, Earl," Uncle Bix shouted.

"Hey, man, I'm just showing him how to chop wood, that's all," Earl said. He grabbed the maul out of my hand. It happened so fast, I couldn't do anything about it. He swung the maul over his head and struck the first and only wedge I'd gotten into the wood. The round split completely, and the wedge thumped onto the ground.

Earl gave me back the maul and said, "That's how it's done."

"Earl, get over here," Gus repeated.

Earl turned and walked back to the car. He pulled a cigarette out of his jeans pocket, put it into his mouth, and lit it. I wondered how a father could let his son, no more than a year or two older than me, smoke those things.

I prayed he would scorch his nose hairs.

"Hey," I said. "You can't smoke that cigarette while my aunt's in the car. She has trouble breathing."

My words stopped Earl in his tracks. He paused, with his back to me for a while, then slowly turned around.

"Earl, you get over here right now. You hear me, boy?" Gus persisted.

Earl ignored him. He held the cigarette out for me to look at. Then he put it between his lips and took a deep drag. He blew out perfect smoke rings and watched them rise into the sky.

"Yeah, right," Earl finally said to his father.

I too watched the rings as they spun upward into nothingness.

Earl walked to the car. Gus sat behind the steering wheel as my uncle helped Aunt Hattie into the back seat. I picked up the maul and watched Earl. He opened the door to the Lincoln Continental and hung on it for a moment as he looked back at me and smiled a wicked smile. Then he flung his cigarette and watched it twirl in the air like an out of control rocket until it landed on the gravel road. He walked over to the smoldering thing and stomped on it with his heel. *That's what I'll do to you someday*, was the silent message. *I'll extinguish you. I'll grind you into nothingness.*

"Get in this car, Earl!" Gus said.

And, for once, Earl did what his father asked.

~ six ~

The nightmare I'd had about losing my hair foretold a real event. The next morning I woke to an awful buzzing sound and the sensation of someone tugging at my scalp. And this time it wasn't a dream.

I sat up stiff and straight and broke lose from the evil-doer. Uncle Bix was kneeling next to my bed. In one hand he held a pair of electric barber shears, no doubt a pair someone had thrown away and he'd repaired. In his other hand was a tuft of my hair. He looked at me and smiled innocently, as if he'd just yanked a splinter out of my thumb.

"What are you doing?" I squealed.

"Making you stronger," he said.

"What?"

"You need your strength today," he said, instructively. "I bought you a new wet suit. You're putting that buoy on that boat."

"But why did you just cut off a clump of my hair?" I complained. "God, I can't believe you did that!"

"Your Aunt Hattie will fix it. She had a beauty shop once, you know."

"But it's *my* hair. How could you just sneak up on me when I'm asleep and cut it like that?"

He stared at me, and frowned. He seemed a little surprised by my anger, as if I'd shown him a side of myself he hadn't believed existed.

I ran my fingers over my scalp and felt a void on the left side. Judging by the amount of hair my uncle held in his fist, I knew I couldn't live with what had just been done to me. He was right. Aunt Hattie would have to fix it.

"You know the story about Samson, right? That story in the Bible," he said.

"Yes, I do. But you've got it *backward*! They cut off his hair to take his strength *away* from him, not to *give* him strength."

He stared off. He looked like someone in a spelling bee who had fifteen seconds to spell a hard word.

"Really?" he said.

I sighed. I wanted to break everything he'd ever repaired in his life.

"Yeah, really," I said. "And after they cut off Samson's hair, they burned his eyes out. Is that next for me? Are you going to burn my eyes out to give me strength?"

He stood up and looked down at me. His face turned serious. "Look," he said. "Around here men wear very short hair. It's for your own good. Just trust me. Like I said, your aunt can fix it."

"I'm not getting a flattop."

"You don't have to have a flattop."

"So what's the alternative—the Marine boot camp look?"

He said nothing and walked off. Again, he seemed a little shocked by my feistiness.

I went into the bathroom and looked at myself in the mirror. My hair looked like a forest that had been clear-cut. The swath of bare skin even exposed the big mole on the right side of my head. I'd never really seen it until now. Sometimes I would poke around the thing when I was bored at school, but my mole had never seen the light of day. It was truly ugly, a brown island of flesh in the shape of Australia.

I closed my eyes and fought back tears. I could hear Aunt Hattie talking to Uncle Bix in the other room. She was not pleased with him, but he didn't try to defend himself. I heard him stomp out of the house. As the vibrations of his steps faded from the cabin, I realized how much my uncle valued Aunt Hattie's opinion, even though he tried not to show it.

She knocked on the bathroom door.

"Don't you worry," she said. She coughed. "I'll make it all right. You'll look just fine. I'll fix it," she said.

Aunt Hattie did fix it. She performed a kind of magic on both the outside and inside of my head. Somehow she even made the mole less conspicuous. She helped me forgive my uncle, and to think differently about what he'd done. Losing my hair was more about him than me, and it would soon grow back anyway. Maybe another part of me would grow along with it.

~ ~ ~

I marched out with my new hairless, mole-exposed head to meet Uncle Bix on the dock. He stood there, the new wet suit draped over his arm. "See, I told you she'd fix it," he said.

He threw me the wet suit and I tried it on.

It fit perfectly.

We jumped into the skiff and traveled across the bay.

"Fits all right, then?" Uncle Bix asked, running his eyes over me as if I were some wrecking-yard engine he was thinking about buying.

"Perfect," I said.

"Your hair looks good," he said.

"What hair?"

"It's for the best," he said. "You just have to trust me on that, Donovan."

He took a deep breath and stared at my mole.

"You know that boy, Earl, you met yesterday?" he said.

"He's not easy to forget," I answered.

"Right, well, he's Gus Hanks's son."

"I figured that."

"You steer clear of him."

"I was planning on it."

"He's always looking for a fight. Always. To tell you the truth, I'm surprised someone hasn't killed him already."

Just then, I was tempted to tell Uncle Bix about Aunt Hattie's opinion of Gus Hanks. I even considered bringing up that old saying, "The apple doesn't fall far from the tree." But I'd made a promise not to repeat what Aunt Hattie had said, and I was going to keep it.

"You feel confident today?" Uncle Bix asked. "The water's going to be deeper, you know. We don't have that low tide like we did before."

"I'll do my best," I said.

We anchored our skiff, and I suddenly realized something. There was really no reason for me to swim down and secure a buoy line to Prometheus. We could just tie an anchor to the buoy and drop her over the side to mark the boat's location. I didn't say anything to my uncle, though. I now understood something about him. He might be a mechanical genius, but he didn't always think things through.

I put on the fins and mask and took hold of the buoy line. Then I sat in the skiff for a bit and stared at the water. For some reason, at that moment, I wanted to ask my uncle why he'd said what he did about the African American woman who'd been killed in the car accident. The time seemed right. I was about to risk my life to help him satisfy this obsession of his. He owed me the truth.

"Uncle Bix," I said.

"What?" he snapped.

"The other night you said it was a good thing that that woman was killed."

"What woman?"

He stared at my fins.

"The black woman who was killed in the car accident."

I'd struck a nerve. "Look!" he shouted. He stood up in the skiff. We almost capsized. "I have my own opinion about those people. And we are just going to leave it at that. All right?"

"Sorry," I said.

I knew it was time for me to shut up and do what we came out here to do. Uncle Bix sat down and stared into the water, almost as if the reflection of himself he was examining wasn't quite right. "Come on," he said. "Let's do this thing."

I rolled over the rail and into the water. I could see better today than yesterday, but Uncle Bix was right. The boat was deeper.

Having a wet suit that fit helped. I could do it. Maybe not on the first try, but I could do it.

I returned to the surface to hyperventilate. Uncle Bix thought I'd given up. He hissed.

"Quitting already?" he said.

"No," I said. "I'm just going to take some deep breaths. I can do it, I think."

His eyes lit up as he watched me inhale and exhale.

"How many of those do you have to take?" he said. "Come on. You said you could do it."

I dove.

I felt strong, confident. I used the fins to thrust my body through the water like a torpedo. I saw the bow of the boat, and the name, Prometheus. Then I felt something holding me back. The line had snagged and coiled into a knot. I was so close, but I had to turn around.

I broke the surface and took a deep breath.

"Well, did you do it?" my uncle asked.

"No. The line got knotted up."

"What? Here, give it to me!"

I threw him the rope. He quickly untangled it. "Darn thing! I knew I should have used the nylon stuff," he muttered. He cast it back to me. I went into my hyperventilating routine again.

"Do you always have to do that?" he whined.

"Yes. I need to oxygenate my blood. It helps. Believe me."

He rolled his eyes.

I dove again.

I pushed harder through the water this time and reached the boat's stern. I tied the line to the rail. I still had plenty of air, so I swam around the port side to the bow and looked for a good place to secure the winch cable, which would be the next feat I had to perform. I saw a big metal cleat on the deck. It would work, I thought.

I ascended, realizing as I rose how inefficiently my uncle had handled things. A better plan would have been to take the cable down at the very beginning, with the buoy secured to the cable line. This would have meant one dive instead of two. Maybe Uncle Bix was purposefully making it hard, testing me. Or maybe he just didn't think things through.

I was nearly out of air as I broke the surface. I was feeling faint and dizzy when I heard my uncle yell out, "You did it, didn't you? You did it!"

"Yeah, I did it! And I found a good place to connect the winch cable."

"That a boy!" he shouted gleefully. He stood and almost capsized the boat again. He punched his closed fist into the air. "That a boy!" he kept saying, cheering me. I treaded water and felt on top of the world. I was safe and warm in the ocean, and I'd just done something big and important for someone.

I'd given life to Uncle Bix's dream.

~ seven ~

Our spirits were high. Securing the buoy line to Prometheus that morning was the first hopeful sign we'd be able to get her up before the summer ended.

That afternoon we celebrated.

No one called it a celebration, it just felt like one. We ate peanut brittle and popcorn, and sat on the porch and looked out at the buoy. Our accomplishment shone on the horizon like a red sun.

"It was the haircut," Uncle Bix said. "He couldn't have done it without the haircut."

He rubbed my scalp, right on top of my mole. Australia burned.

"It was the fact that I had a wet suit that fit," I said.

"Well, anyway, next thing we do is borrow Gus Hanks's winch," my uncle said. "We hook up the cable, then jerk that boat onto this good earth."

"Then what?" I said.

Aunt Hattie was sitting next to me, in that rocking chair she never rocked. She gave me a stern look, as if warning me not to encourage my uncle too much about the boat.

"We lift that Mercruiser 350 out of her, rebuild it, and then stick it in the '63 wooden Chris Craft out back."

Aunt Hattie sighed. The sigh made her cough. Uncle Bix and I stopped talking and just watched her until the coughing ceased.

"Out back?" I asked.

"Right. It's tucked away in the woods behind the cabin," Uncle Bix said. "I bought it for practically nothing."

Aunt Hattie cleared her throat. "You paid way too much for it," she said.

"Three hundred dollars?" he snapped. "You're saying three hundred dollars for a classic wooden boat like a '63 Chris Craft is too much?"

"I'm saying it wasn't really a boat. It was the shell of a boat, and it needs a lot of work. You should have—"

She stopped. She looked out at the buoy. Aunt Hattie knew she was about to say something Uncle Bix wasn't going to like, so she didn't say it. Once again, though, I sensed Aunt Hattie had some kind of special authority over my uncle.

"Well, that's why we're getting that motor out there," Uncle Bix said. "You know what I can do with engines, Babe, don't you?" he said, like a kid asking for a new bike. "And, well," Uncle Bix went on, "it's not just any boat. It's a '63 Chris Craft. They just don't build things like that anymore. It's like a piece of fine jewelry, and I can make it look just like it did when it was made forty years ago. Besides, I have some special plans for it."

"Like what?" I interjected. Uncle Bix waved me off and

gently shook his head. Whatever these special plans were, they were going to be our secret.

Aunt Hattie started coughing again. This time, I wondered if she did it on purpose to get Uncle Bix to stop talking about the boat.

He got up and went over to her. He wrapped his arm around her shoulders. She put her face against his side and covered her mouth. "I need my tank," she said. Uncle Bix went inside to get her oxygen. She stopped coughing as soon as he was gone. She looked at me and said, "Just go along with it. Just let him dream about his boats. All right?"

"All right," I said.

As Uncle Bix returned to the porch, Gus Hanks drove up in that old Lincoln Continental of his. He was alone this time. No Earl, thank God.

Gus got out of the car and waved at us. Only Uncle Bix waved back. "Say your prayers," Aunt Hattie said, as Uncle Bix went out to meet him.

"What?" I said.

"I said say your prayers."

"Why?"

"Because whenever my husband goes out to meet Gus Hanks, it means he's going to be asked to do something he shouldn't."

"Really?"

I stood at the edge of the porch and cocked my ear toward the men's conversation.

"So, you coming to the meeting?" Gus said.

"Where is it?" Uncle Bix replied.

"Where it always is," Gus said. Gus sounded edgy and disappointed. "The old church. Nine o'clock."

"Yeah, well, sure. I'll be there," Uncle Bix murmured.

"Good. It's important. You know that, right?"

"Sure, I know that. I said I'll be there, and I will, Gus."

"Good."

Just before he got into his car, Gus stopped to wave at us, but once again Aunt Hattie ignored him.

Gus drove off. My uncle didn't return to the porch. "I'm going out to the shop to clean up some tools," he said. Then he left Aunt Hattie and me alone.

"He'll never change," Aunt Hattie said.

"What do you mean?" I asked.

She wanted to laugh, but she held it back. "He's not feeling right inside himself about going to that meeting," she said, "and whenever he's feeling like that he retreats to his shop to fix something."

"But he's always fixing something," I said. Aunt Hattie looked at me as if I'd just said something deep, but troubling, like I didn't believe in God. She wasn't disappointed by what I'd said. She was only surprised that I'd been able to think beyond the simple meaning of her words.

After dinner, Uncle Bix left the cabin to walk to Gus Hanks's meeting. Aunt Hattie and I went back to the porch and drank hot chocolate.

"You play checkers?" she asked. She seemed relaxed. I got the feeling she liked being alone with me.

"Yeah," I said.

"Good. After dark we'll go inside and play some."

"Sure," I said.

The evening was quiet and I could hear her breathing, that sound of a chain being dragged over rocks. She had her oxygen tank next to her. I wondered if the night would pass without my having to help her in some way.

"What's this meeting Uncle Bix went to?" I asked.

She sighed.

"They say it's a sportsmen's meeting—but your uncle doesn't hunt or fish," she said. "It's really about something else, I'm afraid. The sportsmen thing is nothing but a front. What's worse, they have these so-called meetings in an old abandoned church. It makes them feel holy, I guess."

"So what's the meeting really about?" I asked.

She looked hard at me.

"Let's just say it's a meeting of small minds, where stupid people talk about stupid things," she said, and followed her words with a half smile.

"Uncle Bix isn't stupid, is he?" I asked.

"No, he isn't, but sometimes he's a little weak at judging people, that's all."

She sat up straight in her rocker.

"I'm afraid your uncle is getting involved with the wrong crowd again," she said.

"Like Gus Hanks?"

"Like Gus Hanks."

"Why?"

"Because your uncle feels in debt to him."

"For money?"

"No, not for money."

"What, then?"

She rubbed her eyes. She was about to say something she knew was true, but she didn't want to admit it.

"His life," she said.

"Really?"

She nodded. "Gus jumped in to protect Bix during a brawl at Steilacoom," she said. "The way Bix tells it, he wouldn't be alive now if Gus hadn't intervened."

I recollected Gus's appearance. He didn't look like a man who'd be tough in a fight. It could have been his easy voice, his soft eyes and round features. But he was a big and stout man. I imagined what it might be like if Santa Claus were driven to rage.

"And," she said, sighing as she spoke, "God knows I hate to say this, but I think your uncle is afraid of him."

"Why?" I asked.

"Because, the way Bix tells it, Gus is a man you dare not cross, or you'll be sorry. Even if he thinks you're crossing him, when you're really not, you'll be sorry."

"How does Uncle Bix know that?" I asked.

She rubbed her eyes.

"Once again, it goes back to their time in Steilacoom," she said. "Bix says Gus was one of those men who believed you were either with him or against him. I don't know the particulars, but you were either Gus's friend or Gus's enemy. There was no in-between. And if you were his enemy, he'd do everything he could to destroy you. No one crossed Gus Hanks."

She looked at the sunset. Her breathing sounded a little better. She reached down and put her hand on my arm. "You know," she said, "your uncle is almost sixty years old, but in many ways he's not much older than you are."

I let her words sink in. I sort of knew what she meant. Sort of.

"I wish he would think a little deeper about things," she continued. "He just jumps in head first with some project without really understanding what it all means. I'm just so worried he'll . . ."

She coughed. I looked at the oxygen tank, ready to grab it and give it to her if she needed it. I thought about what she'd just said, and of my own experiences with Uncle Bix, how he hadn't done a good job in planning how we'd pull the boat up from the bay, how he didn't think things through. I also wondered why, after all these years, Aunt Hattie put up with it.

She stopped coughing and looked at me. She knew I was about to get her oxygen tank, but she stopped me. "Don't worry, I'm all right," she said.

The sun was almost down now. I didn't really want to go inside and play checkers. I wanted to stay outside and keep talking. It was like looking at old photos of close relatives you've never met before.

"Why do you think he did what he did?" I asked.

"You're talking about the robberies?" she replied.

"Yeah."

Her eyes watered.

"I wish I knew the answer to that, Donovan. God, how I wish I knew. We were doing fine there in Seattle. Bix had a good job on the docks. We had a nice little house in a nice little neighborhood. I had my beauty shop. Things were fine. Oh, we didn't have a lot of money, but we were getting by. I guess that wasn't enough for . . ."

Aunt Hattie stopped talking and looked down at her feet, as if she were begging them to take her someplace far beyond where her own strength could take her.

I waited a moment before I spoke.

"Uncle Bix told me he served a longer sentence because he wasn't a snitch."

She lifted her eyes.

"That's right," she said. "Thieves' honor, they call it."

"That makes no sense to me," I said.

"Good," she said.

"I remember the time we went on the boat together to see him."

"Me too," she said. "Bix had been in for about three years, I think. Seemed like forever."

"How many times did you visit him?"

"Every week. Whatever that adds up to."

She coughed some more. I stood up, ready to help her go inside if she wanted. When she stopped coughing, she looked up at me and stared deep into my eyes. "I want to tell you something, Donovan," she said. "I want to give you a piece of advice. Will you listen to me?"

"Yeah, I'll listen."

"The choices you make when you're a young person can stay with you the rest of your life, so you think long and hard before you decide whether to do something or not. You have to live with the decisions you make, so make the right ones. Don't be a fool. You hear me?"

"Yeah," I said.

We were silent for a while. I wondered how deep Aunt Hattie's advice touched her own life. Did she make a mistake in marrying Uncle Bix? Or did it have to do with having chosen to smoke cigarettes for so many years? Or were her words for Uncle Bix himself, for all the bad choices he'd made. I didn't know, but what she'd said before about the broken-down dock serving some sort of purpose made a little more sense to me, like the words on a sign coming into focus as you get closer and closer to it.

"You know," she said. "It's almost pitch-black out here now. I think we should head in."

She stood up and swayed. I put my arm around her to keep her from falling.

"And I think I'll pass on the checkers game. I need to go right to bed," she said.

I helped her into her room. She was very tired, and weak. She lay down and put the oxygen tank next to her on the pillow. I waited until she was asleep and then lifted the mask from her face.

I went back to the porch and sat on the steps. I felt restless. The dangerous old dock beckoned me. The moon was full and I could see the weak spots in the planks. I went out to the dock and made it to the end. It was the first time I'd done it on my own. I sat there awhile and listened to the sounds of the evening. An owl. A chorus of frogs. A breeze cutting through the evergreen trees.

I left the dock and walked up the gravel road to look for the old church where Gus Hanks's meeting was taking place. I told myself I'd walk for about a mile. If I didn't find the church, I'd turn around and go back to the cabin.

The road looked different than it had the day I arrived in the taxi. I'd forgotten that parts of it narrowed into nothing more than an overgrown trail. I walked until I saw a cleared hillside. It was a cemetery. Headstones rose out of tall grass. Sometimes a cemetery means there's church nearby.

I crawled through a barbed-wire fence and walked along the edge of the open field. Headstones poked out of the ground like dull knives. I tried not to step on any graves. I found a good climbing tree, one with thick, low limbs and lots of footholds. Up I went. I climbed about halfway up the tree and looked out. There it was, just on the other side of the hill, a hollowed out church with a dim camp lantern shining at the center of it. Gus Hanks was there. He stood under the light. Seven or eight men huddled around him, including Uncle Bix.

Gus waved his hands as he talked. His son, Earl, wasn't in the huddle, but he was there. He leaned against the wall and looked out the church's broken windows.

He was keeping watch.

I wanted to get closer, but that would mean walking right through the middle of the cemetery. "Don't be a fool!" Aunt Hattie's words rang in my skull, but I headed out anyway. I wanted to hear what they were saying, whether they really were talking about hunting and fishing.

I made it to the middle of the cemetery but still wasn't close enough to hear what Gus was saying. His voice, twisted and hollow sounding, echoed inside the church. I thought I could make out two words, the same two words I'd heard Uncle Bix use, "those people."

I crawled over the grass, keeping my eyes on Earl. Suddenly, he moved away from the wall and closer to the window. He craned that long neck of his and looked outside. With the soft light of the lantern on his face and the huddle of big men behind him, he looked almost younger than me. I wondered why Earl was allowed at the meeting but I wasn't.

I froze.

"Wait," I heard Earl say. His voice broke into the open air. His words were for his father, not me. Gus stopped talking, and Earl said, "I think we have a visitor."

Gus came to the window and stood next to Earl. "Go check it out," Gus commanded.

As Earl made his way to the door, I slithered behind one of the bigger tombstones. The beam of a flashlight scanned the hillside, pausing on some of the stones. It looked as if God were doing it, searching for the names of people he'd decided to send to heaven.

The beam of light grew closer and brighter. I heard footsteps and breathing. I held my breath and closed my eyes.

Finally the light stopped its rise up the hill and began moving from side to side. It held steady for a moment. Things went dark again. Earl had turned around.

I stayed behind the headstone. "Just a deer," I heard Earl say to his father, lying.

Gus Hanks moved back to the huddle of men. Earl returned to the wall. I peered from behind the stone and saw Uncle Bix's face. He was looking right at me. Somehow, I think, he knew I was out here.

Just then, I noticed I was actually facing the tombstone. I'd curled up on top of a person's resting place. The moon partially lit up the stone. "Here lies" were the only words I could read. "Here lies," I whispered to myself. I looked up at the stars. Then I wondered if my own life, and the lives of others, could go anywhere beyond this earth and the time we spend on it. Or is this our one and only chance to do something good?

I didn't know, and I was too tired and afraid to think about it.

~ eight ~

My escape that night ended my good luck for a while.

I arrived home before Uncle Bix. I went in to check on Aunt Hattie. She looked bad, and struggled for every breath.

I stayed next to her bed, ready to help her with the oxygen if she needed it. Finally, near midnight, Uncle Bix returned. Looking tense and impatient, he stomped in.

"What are you doing in here?" he said, when he saw me sitting next to Aunt Hattie. His noisy steps hadn't woken her. I examined his face for any sign that he knew I'd been in the cemetery, hiding behind the gravestone. But his face expressed only one thing now, his worry over Aunt Hattie.

"She seems real bad, so I just . . ." I tried to explain.

"Well, fine, thank you, Donovan," he interrupted.

His voice was tense and calm at the same time. He sat on the bed and took Aunt Hattie's wrist, feeling for her pulse. With his other hand, he brushed her hair away from her forehead and stroked her cheek. His eyes got watery and red. Watching him do this, all the darker things I knew about him, even his presence at Gus Hanks's meeting, seemed unimportant.

"Babe, you need to wake up," he said, in a half whisper. She opened her eyes, lifting her eyelids slowly like the heavy doors of a vault. Then she started coughing. Uncle Bix seemed to take comfort in it, as if her coughing let him know she had some strength left.

"We're going to need to take you to the hospital, Babe," he said. She shook her head back and forth as she continued to cough. "Yes, we do," he said. He looked at me. "Donovan, you go call 911."

"911? Really?" I said.

"Yes!" he barked. "Go! Now!"

Uncle Bix was prepared for these moments. He'd written directions to the cabin on a notepad next to the phone, as if he knew I'd be the one talking to the 911 dispatcher. As I tried to explain to some stranger on the phone why we needed an ambulance to come to our home, I realized Uncle Bix had given me the job as another test of my mettle.

When I went back to the bedroom, Uncle Bix held a little suitcase and stood next to the bed. The suitcase had been packed ahead of time. He'd known this was coming. For once in his life, I thought, he'd planned ahead.

Aunt Hattie lay still on the bed. She'd stopped coughing and was breathing through her oxygen mask.

"Well?" he said. He'd been crying. His eyes were as red as squashed tomatoes.

"They're coming," I said.

"You did good, Donovan. Why don't you go out to the porch and let me know when you see them."

"All right," I said.

I didn't really understand what was wrong with Aunt Hattie. Why, all of a sudden, was she on the verge of dying? I didn't understand how her lung cancer worked against her, only that she had it and that Uncle Bix knew much more about her needs than I did. As I sat waiting on the porch I got angry thinking about how Aunt Hattie wouldn't be suffering like this if she hadn't started smoking cigarettes. It was one of those bad decisions she'd lectured me about. I didn't blame her, though. He life was hard when Uncle Bix was at Steilacoom. Maybe she needed things, like cigarettes, to make life seem easier.

After a few minutes on the porch I walked over to the wood pile and picked up the maul. I had to do something to help me stop feeling so angry. I started splitting wood, and this time I did better. I wished Earl Hanks had been there to see me.

Finally the red light of the ambulance shone in the tree tops as it made its way down the peninsula road. The light was like a meteor moving low through the sky, but fainter. I went back inside to tell Uncle Bix. He was sitting next to Aunt Hattie on the bed. He held her hand.

"They're here," I said.

~ ~ ~

I waited in the lobby while Uncle Bix took care of everything. Aunt Hattie would be admitted, he told me. "Don't worry," he said, just before he left me alone. "We'll bring her back."

I'd lost track of time. What a day it had been. It was two o'clock in the morning, but I wasn't sleepy. I sat by myself in the lobby and looked through magazines, but they were all boring. There was a newspaper in the pile. I hardly ever read newspapers, but I needed something to get my mind off things. The headlines were all about events going on in the world that I didn't understand. Then I came to one that said "Family of Ex–NFL Player Harassed after Moving to Briar's Cove."

The paper talked about how the ex–football player, Sammy Dixon, had moved his family out of Seattle and into a big house on Briar's Cove. It said the Dixons were the first African American family to move into the town. Sammy Dixon had been a lineman for the Seattle Seahawks. He'd been a star prospect and had gotten a big contract, the article said, but had to quit after a couple seasons because of an injured knee. The paper said people had been calling his home and telling him if he didn't move back to the city his house would be burned down.

I stuffed the paper under the magazines when Uncle Bix finally returned to the waiting room. He looked very tired. His face was white. His hands trembled.

"Let's go home and sleep a few hours," he said. "We'll come back later."

I looked up at him. He could tell I didn't want to leave.

"It's for the best," he said.

We took the taxi home and I went right to bed. Uncle Bix went out to his shop. I slept in short spurts, never falling into a deep sleep. At dawn, I went out to the old dock and watched the sun come up. I heard the bark of seals. I saw flocks of seabirds. I looked out over the spot where

Prometheus lay and wondered if Uncle Bix and I would ever return to those waters.

Then I remembered what Uncle Bix had told me about the "better boat" he had hidden in the forest somewhere behind the cabin, the boat we would transplant Prometheus's motor into. I left the dock to explore the woods. I found a well-traveled trail. I walked on it for about a quarter mile until it opened into a clearing. The boat was there.

It rested on stacks of railroad ties. There was sawdust and sawhorses, and lots of carpenter's tools lying around.

The clearing where the boat rested bordered a dry cove. During a very high tide, she could be launched into it, I thought.

The boat was about the same size as Prometheus. The paint had been stripped from her hull, but she had a new cabin and a lot of new planks on deck.

She was nameless.

I climbed onto her. As I sat on her rail, I heard someone drive up the peninsula road. I peered through the trees and saw Gus Hanks's old Lincoln Continental pull up in front of Uncle Bix's shop.

Gus was alone. He was dressed in the same clothes he'd worn at the meeting at the old church. Uncle Bix came out of the shop and walked up to him. I jumped down from the boat and ran back on the trail so I could get close enough to hear what they were saying.

I crouched next to the cabin and listened.

"Yeah, we're going to bring her home today," Uncle Bix said. Gus must have asked him about Aunt Hattie. Uncle Bix's voice was sad and heavy. "She needs to be at home right now," he said.

"That's your business," Gus said coldly. "You still going to be needing my winch and tractor?" he asked.

"Well, yeah, but we'll have to see how things go with Hattie," Uncle Bix replied.

Gus poked at the ground with his boot.

"What the heck you going to do with that sunken motor anyway?" Gus said.

"Put it to use," Uncle Bix said.

So, I thought, Uncle Bix hadn't told Gus about the boat behind the cabin. I wondered why.

"That nephew you got staying with you, he helping you any around here?" Gus asked. His voice was stiff, a little mean.

"Yeah. He's helping me a lot. He's a good kid."

My heart sailed.

"What did you think about what I had to say at the meeting last night?" Gus demanded. He looked around like a scavenging animal does when it eats a carcass in the open.

"I think it's a little too much, Gus," Uncle Bix said.

Gus shook his head and rolled his eyes.

"We can't let those people out here," Gus said. "You've seen what's happened in other places—and you remember what it was like at Steilacoom, how you either stick together or else you—"

"Look, Gus, I've got my mind on other things these days," my uncle interjected. "I'll call you when I'm ready for that winch. All right?"

"Suit yourself," Gus said. Then he got back into his car and drove off.

I sneaked in through the back door. I went to a front window and watched until Gus's car was out of sight. Uncle

Bix came in and saw me standing in the kitchen. He stared at my hands. My palms were dirty.

"Where you been?" he said.

"No where."

He knew I was lying but he didn't care. He went over to the kitchen sink and started washing up.

"I'm going in to the hospital," he said. "And I may not be around much over the next few days. Can I count on you to look after the place while I'm gone?"

In some ways, I thought my uncle's request was selfish. I, too, wanted to see Aunt Hattie. Why shouldn't he take me with him to the hospital? Why should I be left here all alone?

But he had a right to be selfish, I thought, and I'd been sent here to help my aunt and uncle.

"Yeah, sure," I said, and Uncle Bix marched out.

After he left, I went to the end of the old dock. I stared at the red buoy marking the spot where Prometheus was. The buoy seemed bigger, the color brighter. As I watched it bounce on the water, I wondered if what it was tied to was more than just a sunken boat. Was it Uncle Bix's clumsy way of curing Aunt Hattie? Was it his substitute miracle?

I lay down on the planks and thought deeper about these questions. Then I closed my eyes, and felt good knowing I'd been left alone here, to look after things.

~ nine ~

I awoke to the sound of a seagull tapping at the top of one of the pilings. It was trying to mine some sort of insect out of the rotten wood. The gull's beak was too big and blunt for getting at the bug, but it kept on trying until I stood up and scared it off. "Stupid bird," I muttered.

Seeing the gull knock so unsuccessfully at the piling drew my attention to the woodpile near the cabin. Having the pine rounds all split and stacked for Uncle Bix would be a good measure of what I accomplished while he was gone.

I made my way back down the dock. For the first time I didn't have to think much about where to put my feet. I was getting used to it.

It was the middle of the day now. The sun was right overhead, the warmest it had been since I'd come here. At the woodpile I took off my shirt, picked up the maul and the wedges, and started working.

After I'd worked for about an hour, I heard someone or something coming up the road. I hoped it was the taxi returning Uncle Bix from the hospital. But it wasn't. It was Earl Hanks riding one of those BMX bicycles. He skidded to a stop in front of me.

He threw the bike on the ground and stood beside it.

"Still working on that wood, hey?" he said. As always, he smoked a cigarette. Now I liked watching him smoke. He was self-destructing right before my eyes.

"Yep," I said.

I wasn't afraid of him. My dad once told me the best way to deal with a bully is to stand your ground and let him know that even if you lose a fight, you'll still fight and fight hard.

"What do you want?" I said.

"Nothing, really. Just came out here to kick your butt, that's all."

These words helped me understand just what sort of person Earl Hanks was. Earl hardly knew me, yet he wanted to kick my butt. How could someone be so eager to fight a near stranger unless they were angry at the world, unless they hated themselves? It didn't matter what they were fighting for. It was about the fight itself. It was about letting out all the meanness burning inside them.

"What's your problem?" I said.

He rolled his eyes.

"I didn't like the way you ordered me around the other day—you know, how you told me not to smoke with your croaking aunt in my car."

"Get lost," I said.

He stepped forward, then stopped to flick away his

cigarette just as he'd done the other day. He straightened his back.

"It's true, ain't it?" he said.

"What?"

"Your aunt. She's about to croak, ain't she?"

"I said get lost."

Earl sized me up. I could tell he was having second thoughts about fighting me. He could see I was bigger than he was. And, more than anything else, he could tell I wasn't afraid.

"I got a question for you," he said.

I didn't say anything. I just looked at him.

"Why is that crazy uncle of yours trying to pull that rusted old engine out of the bay? What the heck is he going to do with it?"

I shrugged. I was certain now that no one but me, Aunt Hattie, and Uncle Bix knew about the boat in the forest. What I didn't know was why my uncle was keeping it a secret. Why was he keeping it from Gus Hanks? Then, as I looked into Earl's sad, mean face and let him suffer a little with my silence, I remembered what Aunt Hattie had said about Gus. *No one crossed Gus Hanks.* Uncle Bix was hiding the boat because he was afraid Gus might do something to it. He was keeping it away from a man who, deep down, he didn't trust.

"He'll get it running like new," I said. And that's all I would offer.

"Yeah, but what's he going to put it into?" Earl demanded.

I shrugged again. Then I turned my back to him and kept on chopping wood.

"Hey, I asked you a question," Earl said.

"I heard you," I said. I drove the maul into a piece of pine. It broke cleanly. Earl looked down at the split wood. I could tell by the expression on his face that he was reconsidering fighting me.

"Come here," he said.

I put the maul down and walked over to him. I kept my back straight and stared right into his eyes. *If you stand up to a bully, chances are he'll back down . . .*

I was a few inches from his face. "I'm here," I said. "What do you want?"

He laughed, but it was a fake laugh. I held my stare. He had to look up at me. His gaze passed over my head to the sky. He glanced at the sun. "You know," he said, "it's too hot for a fight. We'll do it some other day."

"I'll be here," I said.

He turned and walked off toward his bike. He lit another cigarette, drew hard on it and pushed out the smoke as if his mouth were a volcano.

I watched him ride off. I felt good about what I'd done, but I was sad at the same time. Though Earl and I hadn't come to blows, his words had hit me hard.

Your aunt. She's about to croak, ain't she?

~ part two ~

Raising Prometheus

~ ten ~

Two weeks passed, and we entered the first days of July. I never told Uncle Bix about my run-in with Earl Hanks.

Uncle Bix had enough to worry about.

He was gone most of the time. He was at the hospital with Aunt Hattie practically all day, every day. I tried to stay busy. I called my mom and dad every morning. Dad wasn't pleased with my being alone in the cabin, but he wasn't angry enough to bring himself to talk to my uncle about it.

The last time I was on the phone with Dad, I'd asked about my twin sisters, The Two H's. In a weird way, I missed them. I could hear them fighting in the background. Dad let out a sigh and said, "Well, they are what they are." He had to hang up and separate them before they killed each other. "Be safe, son," he said, instead of good-bye.

I worked hard on the woodpile. I finished splitting and stacking it. Then I visited the boat in the forest and started setting new deck planks in place. It was the first time I'd really worked at building something with wood, and it was a challenge. I managed to get a few planks down, though many of them weren't lined up straight. I hoped Uncle Bix would at least give me some credit for trying.

Finally, early in July, Uncle Bix and I went together to visit Aunt Hattie. Twice, in two days, he took me along. She looked bad, but she tried to pretend she wasn't as sick as she really was. The day before we were going to bring her home Uncle Bix told me, "It's up to us to make her better. She won't let those doctors do anything," he said. "It's up to us."

There was real hope in Uncle Bix's voice that day. We worked together on cleaning the cabin and getting it ready for Aunt Hattie's return. Uncle Bix even cooked up some meals and stuck them in the freezer so we'd have food ready to heat up.

The next morning, just before we left to get Aunt Hattie, I asked Uncle Bix to follow me out to the Chris Craft in the woods so I could show him what I'd done. "You been working on it?" he said, as we traveled the trail. He seemed half mad, half happy.

"Yeah," I said. "I needed something to do."

He smiled, something he hadn't been doing much of lately. His whole face seemed to break apart.

When we reached the boat, he hopped onto her deck and ran his gaze over all the new wood I'd put down. It wasn't much, and in some ways my work looked a little sloppy. But, it seemed, Bix could ignore the places where I'd made mistakes. He focused on the good parts. "Where'd you learn to do that?" he said.

"Maybe I inherited it from you," I replied. This delighted

him. It was as if he suddenly realized how closely related we were. He examined my face, trying to see himself in it. He patted me on the head. "There's still a lot of work to do," he said, "but I want you to know I appreciate this, Donovan."

We walked to the bow. Uncle Bix ran his palm along the rail and peered out into the forest as if it were an ocean, and he, Aunt Hattie, and I were bucking big waves, on our way to discovering a new continent. Seeing him like this made me think of what he'd told Aunt Hattie, that he had "special plans" for the Chris Craft. Before I could ask him what those plans were, he told me.

"Someday," he said, "before the end of this summer, I want to take your Aunt Hattie for a ride on this vessel."

"That would be great," I said.

He patted my shoulder.

"Yes," he said. "Great."

We hiked back to the cabin and waited for our taxi. All during the ride, a heavy sadness seemed to hang in the air, as if everyone in the world knew something bad was about to happen and there was nothing we could do about it.

Things brightened a little when we got to Aunt Hattie's hospital room. She looked better than she had the day we'd brought her there. She was wearing a long blue dress and earrings and lipstick. She'd brushed her hair and put some pins in it.

She was sitting on the edge of her bed when we came in. She stood and swayed. Uncle Bix took her elbow and steadied her. "It's about time you got here," she said.

Uncle Bix slid his hand down Aunt Hattie's elbow and took her wrist. Then a nurse entered. She was a small African American woman. Her white uniform made her skin seem blacker. She had big eyes and tiny hands. Her voice was like a bell ringing in the distance.

"Is this that nephew you've been talking about?" she asked Aunt Hattie.

"That's him," Aunt Hattie replied.

"Well, what a handsome boy," the nurse said.

"Donovan," Aunt Hattie said, shifting her eyes from me to the nurse, "if it weren't for this woman here, I might not be standing and talking to you right now. It's just a miracle, the way she fixed me up."

Before I could say anything, the nurse stepped forward and waved Aunt Hattie off.

"Oh, stop it now," she said. "You're standing and talking because you're one tough lady."

"I'm not *that* tough," said Aunt Hattie.

"Sure you are, Babe," Uncle Bix said.

All this time, my uncle had been standing like some kind of barrier between the nurse and Aunt Hattie. When he spoke, Aunt Hattie pulled away from him. She slipped her arm out of his grip and stared hard into her husband's eyes.

"No!" she said. "I am *not!*"

For some reason, Uncle Bix looked at me, as if he were trying to retreat into the safety of my young face. He seemed to be asking me what he should do now.

I couldn't help him.

"It doesn't matter, does it?" the nurse said. "Because all we care about is that you're better than the day you came here," she continued. "And you're going home."

I'll never in my life forget what happened next. I stepped back and leaned against Aunt Hattie's bed. I looked at her, and at Uncle Bix. All the hard times they'd experienced over the years seemed to be pressing into this clumsy moment. Uncle Bix stood there between Aunt Hattie and the nurse and couldn't think of anything to say.

The nurse seemed to feel what I felt. She lowered her head and went to the edge of the room, trying to make herself invisible. There was some sort of medical machine there, something with lots of knobs and gauges that must have been hooked up to Aunt Hattie at some point. The nurse leaned over the machine and began working on it. Her tiny hands moved quickly, but perfectly, as she adjusted all the dials and switches. Uncle Bix watched every movement of her hands. Aunt Hattie watched Uncle Bix, and I knew he could feel her stare upon him. He went over to the nurse, who continued working on the machine. She stopped and looked up when Uncle Bix touched her.

He put his fingers on her bare, black arm, resting them there lightly as if her skin were hot. I looked at Aunt Hattie. She stared at Uncle Bix's hand, at the scars on his knuckles.

"I want to thank you," Uncle Bix said to the nurse. He looked right into her eyes. She smiled a big smile. Her teeth were large and beautiful.

"You are welcome, Mister Sanger," the nurse said. "Now, you take good care of that great lady of yours, you hear me?"

"Yes, I hear you," Uncle Bix said.

The nurse nodded her approval, and turned to the doorway, where a tall orderly leaned over a wheelchair, inviting Aunt Hattie to sit in it. The wheelchair looked shiny and new. Some flowers rested in the corner of the seat.

"Your ride is here, lady," the nurse said, smiling again.

The room was quiet. No one moved. Then I lifted myself from Aunt Hattie's bed and picked up her suitcase from the middle of the floor.

"Let's go home," I said.

We were back at the cabin by early afternoon. The trip wore out Aunt Hattie. She went right to bed, taking her oxygen tank with her.

Uncle Bix and I silently ate our lunch on the porch. The whole time we kept looking out at the red buoy. Without speaking, we somehow knew we were both asking the same question: Would we ever be able to work again at raising Prometheus?

There were other questions, but they were locked away inside Uncle Bix's head, where I couldn't reach them. I could tell, by the way he just looked blankly out to sea, that something else was bothering him. He sat like a statue, his hands cupped over his knees, his back straight, as if he were in a staring contest with the ocean. He didn't blink, and breathed in a slow, deep rhythm. I wanted to ask Uncle Bix what was troubling him. I wondered if it had something to do with the nurse in Aunt Hattie's hospital room, if she'd made Uncle Bix think about things so differently it had thrown his world out of balance.

It took Aunt Hattie's voice to jerk Uncle Bix back to life. I didn't know she was capable of shouting like that, but it was her all right. "Donovan, come in here. Just you," she said.

I looked at Uncle Bix for approval. He rubbed his eyes, waking from his paralyzing thoughts. "Well, go ahead," he mumbled.

She was lying still in the bed when I came in. She took off

the oxygen when she saw me. She patted the mattress next to her leg. "Sit here," she said.

Some life came back to her face when I sat next to her. She looked me right in the eyes and said, "I don't know if what your uncle is planning on doing with that sunken motor is really worth anything . . ." She coughed. ". . . but I want . . . I want you to help him do it. I want you and your uncle to pull up that boat out there and get that motor out of her. That . . . that . . ."

She went into a frenzy of coughing. I thought for sure it would bring in Uncle Bix, but it didn't. Maybe he'd fallen back into the pit of his troubling thoughts, or maybe he understood that this was a private and special time for me and Aunt Hattie.

She finally stopped and began to breathe steadily again. She put the oxygen mask over her face. I waited patiently for her to speak. "That would make me very happy," she said. A faint glow of color seeped into her cheeks. "Getting that boat up, I mean."

"All right," I said. "We'll do it."

And she fell asleep.

~ eleven ~

Somehow Uncle Bix seemed to know what Aunt Hattie had told me, and it lifted his spirits. The next day, during low tide, we returned to the red buoy. This time we took the winch cable with us.

I sat wearing my wet suit, mask, and fins in the bow of the skiff, more determined than ever to reach Prometheus. The sun had just come up, and there was a long line of red clouds on the horizon. "Red sky at morning, sailor take warning," Uncle Bix said. "We better get this done in a hurry."

"Is that saying really true?" I asked. I was ready to flop into the water. Uncle Bix sighed. He seemed to know this would be the first in a long line of questions I'd ask before plunging in.

"Not really," he said. "But it's best to err on the side of caution."

"You didn't listen to the weather report?"

"No, I didn't listen to the weather report."

"Don't you think we should do that before we—"

"What I think is this, Donovan. I think you should stop talking and get into the water. Don't let that cable get wrapped around your legs. It's heavy. It'd be hard to shake it loose."

"Shouldn't we have used a thinner cable? I mean . . ."

"We are pulling up a boat from the bottom of the ocean, Donovan. We need a heavy cable. Please, get in the water."

I dove in. The current was stronger than it was the last time. I couldn't see very well. I swam down to the boat, but I had a hard time finding the cleat on the bow. The current kicked up sand. I rose to the surface.

"Well?" Uncle Bix said.

I showed him the end of the cable. He hissed and shook his head. "What's wrong?" he asked.

"There's a current. The water's cloudy. I can't see too well."

"So, what are you telling me? Should we come back some other time, or what?"

"No. I think I can do it. I found the cleat. Just one more dive. That's all I need."

As I treaded water, I felt the weight of the cable pulling me down. I looked toward the cabin as I took some deep breaths. I saw a car drive up. It was a new, white car, a car like a government official might drive. "Somebody just drove up in front of the cabin," I said. Uncle Bix turned sharply to look. "Who is it?" I asked.

A man in a suit got out. He had neatly combed brown hair and wore sunglasses, even though the sun was barely up.

"I don't know," said Uncle Bix, but I had the feeling he really *did* know and wasn't telling me.

"He's going to bother Aunt Hattie, isn't he?" I said. I was getting a little tired treading water while holding the cable. Uncle Bix noticed this, and said, "Look, Donovan, he's probably just some salesman. He'll knock on the door a couple times and then leave. Your Aunt Hattie won't even get out of bed, believe me. Now get in the water and attach that cable."

I dove. I went straight for the cleat on the bow. The current had died down a little and I moved through the water easier than before. I wrapped the cable around the cleat and popped back up. "Done!" I said.

"That a boy!" Uncle Bix said.

I looked past him to the cabin. The visitor had already knocked on the door and was walking back to his car.

"Look," I said. "He's leaving."

Uncle Bix sighed. He wanted to pretend the visitor wasn't there.

"Well, so he is," Uncle Bix said. "Come on. Get back into the skiff. You did a good job. This afternoon I'll call Gus and tell him to bring his winch and flatbed over."

The man got into his car and slowly drove away. Uncle Bix watched him out of the corner of his eye as I climbed back into the skiff. We drifted for a while. Uncle Bix wanted to make sure the visitor was long gone before he started the motor and alerted the stranger to our whereabouts. I decided to take advantage of the situation. Uncle Bix wanted to stay out on the water until the visitor was gone. We were all alone out here, where nobody else could hear us. It was the perfect time to ask Uncle Bix about his "sportsmen" meetings.

"What was that meeting about you went to the other night?" I asked.

His face tightened. If I hadn't done such a good job with the cable, I think he would have yelled at me and told me to mind my own business. Instead he said, "It's a sportsmen's meeting. That's all."

"What kind of sports do you talk about?"

"Hunting, fishing, that kind of thing."

I watched the visitor's car move up the peninsula road. I hoped he'd travel slow so Uncle Bix and I would have more time to talk.

Then it happened again. Words just spilled out of my lips.

"Why did you do what you did—the robberies, I mean?"

"What?" Uncle Bix growled.

"The robberies. Why'd you do it?"

He stared at me for a moment, and then said, "Hard to say. Guess I wanted more things, and I couldn't get those things making an honest living."

"What things?"

"Well, my own shop, for one. Always wanted my own shop."

"What else?"

He shrugged. Whatever the things were, they didn't seem to matter to him anymore.

"What was it like in prison?" I said.

Uncle Bix smiled a half smile.

"You really want to know?" he asked.

I nodded. I watched the visitor's car. *Go slow. Please, go slow.*

"It's terrible. You live like an animal in a cage. You wait. You count the days. You trust nobody," he said.

I didn't say anything, but I thought about how Uncle Bix's time in prison was kind of like walking down the old dock and trying not to fall through. Uncle Bix seemed to realize I was thinking about what he'd just said, and I think he was pleased I was considering his words so seriously. We sat silent for a time. Both of us watched the visitor's car as it made its way to the paved county road, then sped up and shrank in the distance.

~ twelve ~

Gus Hanks didn't keep his promise. It turned out the winch he'd said Uncle Bix could use was broken, and Uncle Bix would have to fix it before he could borrow it.

But it didn't matter. That red sky we'd seen in the morning really did mean a storm was coming in. The weather was bad for three days. Getting Prometheus onto the dry dock Uncle Bix had made out of railroad ties would have to wait.

During the storm, Uncle Bix spent his time over at Gus's place. He worked on the winch under a tarp tent until he got it running good again, not like brand new, but good enough to do the job.

While Uncle Bix was gone, I kept a close watch on Aunt Hattie. Sometimes she seemed better. Other times she seemed on the verge of death. Once, I almost called 911.

During the good times, she asked a lot about the boat. Talking about it was like medicine for her. Color would return to her face and she'd straighten up as if she were looking for something on the horizon.

"So, you got the cable hooked up, right?" she asked one afternoon.

"Yep," I said. We were in her bedroom, but she was sitting in a chair. The oxygen tank was on her lap.

"Good. So we just need that winch," she said.

"Yep. Uncle Bix is almost done with it."

"God, I despise that man," she said.

"Uncle Bix?"

"No, of course not. Gus Hanks. He's nothing but a bigoted phony."

Aunt Hattie started coughing. This gave me time to think about whether I should say what I wanted to say. I handed her the oxygen mask and watched her eyes. Then I said it.

"I went to that meeting of theirs," I said. She jerked the mask off her mouth.

"*What?*" she said.

"Well, I mean, I wasn't inside with them or anything. I just looked through a window from behind a gravestone."

"Behind a gravestone?"

"Yeah, at that old cemetery nearby. I could see—"

"Donovan!" she interrupted. "Please, don't do a crazy thing like that again. You hear me?"

"But—"

"Just don't!" she snapped.

The emotion I'd raised in her was tiring her out. I felt guilty about it. She put on the mask and struggled to breathe.

I changed the subject back to the boat.

"I think we're going to pull up Prometheus tomorrow."

She nodded. I could tell she was smiling under the oxygen

mask. She lifted her hand and pointed to my hair. She took the mask away and said, "You need a trim."

"A trim?" I squealed. My hair had grown about half an inch since I'd gotten the terrible flattop.

"Yes," she said. Her face was stern. "Go get my clippers. They're in that dresser drawer over there."

She pointed. It was hard for her to raise her arm. How would she be able to cut my hair, I wondered.

I got the clippers and handed them to her. She sat up and turned them on. She studied the moving teeth to make sure they were working right. "You just sit on the floor there," she said. "Lean your back against the mattress. Sit up straight now, so I don't have to bend over too much."

Somehow she managed to do it. It didn't matter to me that I was losing my hair again. I liked the feel of it. I closed my eyes and let my aunt try to protect me in the only way she knew how.

It took almost half an hour for Aunt Hattie to finish my haircut. She had to stop often to rest and draw on her oxygen tank. But afterward, she seemed all right. She even made a joke about it. "That was the most strenuous haircut I've ever given in my life," she said.

She fell asleep. I left her alone and went out to the old dock to wait for Uncle Bix to return from Gus's place. The storm had passed. I was anxious to find out about the winch. Finally I saw Gus and my uncle drive up in the old Lincoln Continental. Uncle Bix got out and Gus drove away.

Uncle Bix went right into the cabin. I followed behind him. Inside, I saw him peering into the bedroom to check on Aunt Hattie. He quietly closed the door and turned to me. "The winch is fixed," he said. "Tomorrow, we pull up the boat."

He looked at my hair as he spoke. His eyes filled with delight. There was a lot to be happy about. We had a winch, and I'd gotten a haircut without being ordered to.

There was a knock on the front door. I looked out the window and saw the man who'd come by while we were out in the skiff. Now I knew that this stranger, whoever he was, wasn't "just some salesman."

Uncle Bix waited for the man to knock again before he said, "Look, Donovan, why don't you go out back and lay down some more decking in the old Chris Craft."

"All right," I said. I knew Uncle Bix wanted to be alone with his visitor. He must have wanted it real bad to trust me with laying more decking in the Chris Craft.

"And go out the back door, would you?" he added.

I waited to answer. I wanted to ask Uncle Bix why he was so anxious to get rid of me. But I didn't.

"Okay," I muttered.

I left the cabin but waited just outside to listen.

They spoke a few words at the front door and then went into the living room. I could hear only pieces of their conversation. I heard the visitor say the name of the African American football player, Sammy Dixon. I heard him say Gus Hanks's name. I heard him use the word arrest. I heard Uncle Bix say "No." Over and over again, "No . . . No . . . No . . .," he kept saying.

Uncle Bix and the stranger moved to another room. Now I couldn't hear them at all. I stayed on my knees and crawled around to the front of the cabin. The stranger's car was parked close to the porch. I decided to look inside.

I stayed on my knees until I reached the passenger side. Peering through the window I saw a big radio right in the middle of the dashboard and a microphone hitched to it. There were metal handcuffs on the seat, next to a folder left sprawled open like a gutted fish. Two photographs lay on top of the other papers in the folder. The photos were of different men, both of them in prison outfits. The pictures were taken from the chest up, and though the men were younger and looked a little different than they did now, I recognized them. One was Gus Hanks. The other was Uncle Bix.

I pulled back from the car window when I heard Uncle Bix and the stranger's voices coming toward me from inside the cabin. I crawled around the front bumper and hid behind the trunk of a tree. Then I crouched down and crawled onto the path leading to the boat. I stopped to watch the visitor get in the car, reach over and close the folder on the seat, and then drive off. My heart rose in my chest and my face turned hot. I didn't know *who* the man was, but I did know *what* he was. He was a police officer, and he was questioning my uncle about something. What's more, he'd come in just as Gus Hanks had left. The two may have passed each other on the way, and I was afraid of what might happen because of it.

~ thirteen ~

Once again, Gus didn't keep his word. Uncle Bix had fixed the winch, but Gus didn't bring it by the cabin until almost a week later. Me and Uncle Bix were getting worried. It was past the middle of July, and we were heading into the last half of the summer.

Finally the day came, and things looked promising. We had clear skies. The tide was low and the water was flat.

There was one wart on the face of the day, though. Earl came with Gus when he brought by the winch. This time Earl didn't pay much attention to me. *If you stand up to a bully. . .*

The winch was mounted on a big flatbed truck with double tires in the back. It looked like a tow truck. Uncle Bix said it was more or less his own design. It looked like a giant insect made out of metal, with wheels.

Uncle Bix drove the contraption close to the water. Gus and Earl stood next to it, but were going to let me and

Uncle Bix do all the work. I think they'd come just to see if we'd fail, so they could laugh at us.

I stood next to the truck. I heard a knocking sound coming from the cabin. I looked over and saw Aunt Hattie through the window of her bedroom. She was sitting on the edge of her bed and using her cane to tap against the glass. Uncle Bix followed my gaze. Then he panicked.

He'd been standing on the bed of the truck. He jumped down and ran to the cabin. I followed him. Earl laughed. I wanted to pull his nose off.

Aunt Hattie was lying down when we reached her. "What's wrong, Babe?" Uncle Bix howled.

She turned away from him and looked out the window at the winch. "I want to be out there," she said. Her voice was soft, but determined. There wasn't any way we were going to change her mind. She was going outside.

"We can't have you do that, Babe," Uncle Bix said. "You're not strong enough."

"The heck I'm not!" she said. The force of her voice was meant to convince him she was up to it. "You just sit me on the porch where I can see," she said. "I'll be all right."

She put on her oxygen mask. Uncle Bix looked at me. Without saying anything, he signaled me to help lift Aunt Hattie out of bed and guide her to the porch. She did better than I thought. She really wanted to see us raise Prometheus.

"Go get a wool blanket to put over her legs," Uncle Bix told me.

"*No*," Aunt Hattie spouted. "I'm fine. It's a beautiful, warm day. I'm fine. You two just go do your job."

We returned to the winch and the flatbed and connected

the cable. I watched Earl out of the corner of my eye. He left the beach and snuck off behind the cabin, lighting a cigarette along the way.

"Go ahead and put some blocks under the tires," Uncle Bix said. He was too focused on the job to notice Earl. "Did you hear me?" he said.

"Yeah, sorry," I said. I jumped down from the truck and pulled over some cinder blocks to jam under the back tires. I searched for Earl. He was out of sight. What if he found the trail leading to the Chris Craft, I thought?

"All right, then," said Uncle Bix. His voice rang with excitement. "Let's pull her up."

We climbed into the cab of the truck. That's where the controls were, and Uncle Bix wanted us inside just in case the cable snapped. The winch started turning. It groaned and squeaked. The cable tightened, and in just moments we saw Prometheus breach the water like a wooden whale.

My eyes went back and forth from the boat to Aunt Hattie. Life and color returned to her face as the boat rose out of its watery grave.

"I knew it!" said Uncle Bix. "I knew she'd slide right along on that sandy bottom." He punched his fist into the air.

Gus came a little closer to watch. Now that things were going according to plan, he wanted to be part of the action. Earl was nowhere to be seen.

"You're not home free yet," Gus said. He just couldn't believe things were working out as planned. "She might slam into some drift logs. There's some out there, you know."

"Nope," said Uncle Bix defiantly. "She's on a clear path. I mapped it out during low tide. My only worry is if her bow pushes too much sand up and she bogs down on us."

It was good to hear Uncle Bix argue with Gus. I wondered if things were changing between them.

I watched as Prometheus came completely out of the water. Her bow cut like a plow through the sandy shore.

"Look at that!" Uncle Bix said. He gazed at Aunt Hattie and pointed to the boat. "We got her, Babe! We got her!"

Aunt Hattie gave him a thumbs up and smiled.

"All right," said Uncle Bix. "Now we get her onto the railroad ties."

The structure Uncle Bix had built with the ties was farther away from the beach, closer to the cabin, almost right next to Uncle Bix's shop. He called his structure "the rack." This is where we'd work on Prometheus over the rest of the summer.

"We'll slack off on the cable and drive the winch around behind the rack. Then we'll pull her right onto it," he said.

I searched again for Earl. Now I knew for certain he was on the trail and had probably found the boat in the woods. I hoped I was wrong.

We positioned the winch behind the rack and started winding up the cable again. Everything worked perfectly. In about fifteen minutes, Prometheus was mounted nice and even on the railroad ties.

"She looks better than I thought she would," Uncle Bix said. "Except for the hole in the starboard bow that sunk her, she's got some decent wood left in her," he said.

He was right. The boat was in pretty good shape for having been under water a year or so.

"Naagh," Gus growled. I wanted to turn him into concrete. "She's dry-rotted down to her ribs. Motor's probably shot," he said.

"We'll see," I said. Gus didn't like my words. I hadn't

really contradicted him, but my saying anything at all about the subject seemed to irritate him a little. He shook his head and waved me off. I looked over at Aunt Hattie. She was so happy she was crying.

"Okay, Gus," Uncle Bix said. He'd disconnected the cable from the winch and jumped down from the flatbed. "You can have her back now. Thank you," Uncle Bix added.

Gus kept shaking his head. "Yeah, well, you got yourself a pipe dream going here, Bix," he said. "But it's your foolish business, not mine."

Gus walked around the side of the truck and was ready to get in when he noticed Earl was missing. He stopped, looked around, and then said to Uncle Bix, "You seen the boy?" There was worry in his voice.

"Nope," Uncle Bix said. Just then Earl came around the side of the cabin. He'd had enough time to go into the woods and find the old Chris Craft before coming back. He had an evil smile on his face.

"Where you been?" Gus yelled. Earl shrugged.

"Just snoopin' around," Earl said. He took a cigarette and some matches out of his shirt pocket. He struck a match and stared at the flame. He wanted me to stare at it, and I did. He walked over to a burn barrel near the porch. He flicked the match into it.

"Hey," I shouted. "What the heck are you doing?"

The trash in the barrel ignited. Flames soon billowed over the metal rim.

"Never mind," said Uncle Bix, softly. I was ready to pounce on Earl, but Uncle Bix held me back. "That trash needed burning anyway," he said.

~ fourteen ~

The next three or four weeks were the best of my life. The rest of July and the first part of August blessed us with a stretch of warm, clear days. Aunt Hattie seemed better. Every day, as Uncle Bix and I dug into the heart of Prometheus, she watched from the porch.

We spent almost all our time on the motor. Uncle Bix taught me a few simple things along the way, like always using the proper tool, measuring things twice, and never overtightening a bolt or a screw.

We completely dismantled the Mercruiser, spreading the parts all over Prometheus's deck. There were hundreds of pieces—washers, bolts, nuts, springs, gaskets, and strange looking things only Uncle Bix could identify. I was certain he wouldn't remember where all the parts belonged after he'd cleaned and fixed them all.

We didn't spend as much time on the Chris Craft. With

Prometheus out of the sea and onto "the rack," Uncle Bix had become a kid with a new toy.

"I've never seen him so determined," Aunt Hattie said one afternoon. I'd taken a break while Uncle Bix continued to work on the engine. It was a hot day. Aunt Hattie and I sat on the porch drinking iced tea from pickling jars. She wore shorts and a straw hat. She let the sun beat on her knees. She was getting better. She was really getting better.

"Do you think he'll be able to do it?" I asked. I watched Uncle Bix as he stood on deck with his hands on his hips, staring down at the complicated array of parts at his feet.

"Do what?" she said.

"Put all those parts back together."

"Of course," she said. "He's a genius when it comes to that sort of thing. People use that word too much these days. But with Bix it's the right word."

Aunt Hattie's voice was so clear and strong that I couldn't help but think a miracle had taken place. I remembered how she herself had used that word when she thanked the nurse at the hospital. It was true. I hadn't heard her cough all morning and she hadn't brought out the oxygen tank. She looked ten years younger.

"Maybe he should have been an engineer for NASA or something," I said. I kept my eyes on Uncle Bix. He'd picked up one of the parts and was studying it, rolling it around in his fingers, like a jeweler staring at a rare stone.

"Maybe," Aunt Hattie said, her voice trailing off in disappointment. "But we can't turn back the clock, now can we. You remember what I told you about choices, right?"

"Yeah."

She watched Uncle Bix's fingers just as I did. "Your

uncle's problem, Donovan, was that he let other people make his choices for him. He hasn't been his own man. He gets swept up in somebody else's initiative instead of finding his own. You promise me you won't do that, all right? You be your own man."

"All right."

At that very moment, as if some supernatural being was playing tricks on us, Gus drove up. He was alone. He got out of his car, waved at me and Aunt Hattie, and went over to Uncle Bix.

"Doggone it!" Aunt Hattie said. I'd never heard her speak with such spunk. "Why doesn't he just disappear or something?" she said.

Uncle Bix put down the part he was working on and jumped over the rail of the boat to meet Gus.

"Another meeting?" I said.

"I'm afraid so," Aunt Hattie replied. "And don't you get any ideas about sneaking off to it," she said.

I tried to listen in on Gus and Uncle Bix's conversation, but I couldn't hear what they were saying. Aunt Hattie watched their mouths, trying to read their lips.

Gus patted Uncle Bix on the shoulder. Uncle Bix stared at Gus's hand as if it were the droppings of a giant bird. Uncle Bix nodded, and then Gus walked back to his car. He waved at us again, got in the car, and drove off.

"Pray that your uncle will be strong," Aunt Hattie said. She coughed for the first time all day.

I looked off and tried to gather enough courage to say what I wanted to say, knowing Aunt Hattie might not like hearing it.

"Some man has come to visit Uncle Bix," I said. I didn't

want to get Aunt Hattie too excited by telling her I thought the man was a cop. Still, the way I spoke the word alerted her that this was no ordinary person. She stuck her chin out and narrowed her eyes, as if she were trying to stare down a mean dog.

"What did he look like?" she asked.

"Kind of tall, brown hair, narrow face, wearing sunglasses. He was driving—"

"I don't know who he is," she interrupted. "And don't you worry about it!"

She looked at me as if suddenly I'd become that mean dog she was trying to stare into submission. "Okay," I said. "I won't worry about it."

Uncle Bix climbed back into Prometheus. He looked up at us and frowned. He seemed to know what we were talking about, and he could tell Aunt Hattie wasn't happy with him. He dug into the motor again, as if getting the thing running was all he'd have to do to make things right with her.

~ ~ ~

That night, Aunt Hattie tried to prepare dinner for us—pork roast with mashed potatoes and coleslaw. She tried to finish but had to quit before everything was done. "You can manage the rest of it," she said, shuffling off to bed. Uncle Bix put her tank next to her. Seeing her lying there made me wonder if the miracle was over, or if it had ever happened in the first place.

Uncle Bix and I ate dinner together. He was in a hurry, and in a bad mood.

"Maybe tomorrow we'll go back to the Chris Craft in the woods," he said. "There's lots to do with her yet."

"Yeah," I said.

We failed at finishing the cooking. The potatoes weren't done all the way. The pork was burned on the outside but almost raw in the middle.

"So, you going somewhere tonight?" I asked.

"Yes. I am. Why?"

"One of those meetings?"

"Yes. 'One of those meetings.'"

"One of those *sportsmen* meetings?"

He looked fiercely at me. He didn't like the way I said that word, "sportsmen." He knew I knew it was a lie.

"That's right," he said.

I was silent, and noticed the same feeling in the pit of my stomach as when I'd stood up to Earl Hanks. I knew I was taking a chance in pressing Uncle Bix. If I pressed too hard he might never answer any of my questions again. But something inside me told me I had to do it, just like I had to stand up to Earl. If I didn't, who would?

I took a deep breath and said, "Do you know about that thing with the football player's family?"

Uncle Bix's eyes darted toward me and then quickly away again.

"I know there's some washed-up lineman who's moved into Briar's Cove," Uncle Bix said. I was surprised he'd answer my question at all.

"But I mean that bad stuff that's going on with his family," I said.

"What bad stuff?"

"Some people are harassing them because—"

"Listen," Uncle Bix said, cutting me off, "I've got enough troubles of my own right now, Donovan. I can't take on somebody else's troubles, all right?"

I was quiet, wondering why Uncle Bix had chosen to say he was "taking on" somebody else's troubles.

"Look," he said. He wanted to change the subject. "I want you to stay close to your Aunt Hattie tonight. I know she's been doing better, but I think she pushed herself way too hard today."

I nodded, but didn't say anything. I wanted to ask Uncle Bix about the stranger who'd come to our house, but now wasn't the time. I could tell he'd had enough of my questions, enough of me.

I finished my dinner while Uncle Bix got ready to leave. He said good-bye to Aunt Hattie but not to me. I went to the porch and watched him head up the road. He walked with his head down.

I went back in to check on Aunt Hattie. Uncle Bix was right—she'd pushed herself too hard. She was sound asleep, breathing heavily. Her face was white as milk.

I called my dad. As usual, I could hear The Two H's bickering in the background. Dad had to pull away from the telephone to yell at them. I tried to tell him about Prometheus, how we'd succeeded in getting the boat up, and that Uncle Bix had started to fix the motor. But, like last time, Dad wanted to talk about only me or Aunt Hattie. Whenever I mentioned Uncle Bix, Dad changed the subject. "You just keep us updated on your Aunt Hattie," he said. Again I wondered how two brothers could hate each other that much.

It was almost dark when I finished talking to Dad. I

walked out to the old dock to watch the sunset. I could now get to the end of the wood easily. I'd mastered it.

I went back to the cabin while there was still some daylight left. The phone was ringing as I stepped inside. I answered it and a man asked for "Mister Bix Sanger." The voice sounded familiar. Was it the stranger who'd visited us? I told him Uncle Bix wasn't home. He asked when he'd be back. I told him I didn't know. He didn't leave a message, and he wouldn't give me his name when I asked for it.

I stood in the kitchen, thinking hard about what I should do. I had an awful feeling that Uncle Bix was getting himself into trouble again. If he did, it would be the worst thing that could happen—not only to him, but to Aunt Hattie.

As I stood there I could hear Aunt Hattie breathing. It was that terrible sound of a chain being dragged over rocks, but now the rocks were sharp and jagged, the chain old and rusty.

I went into the living room, to the copper bin next to the woodstove. It probably held kindling during the fire-burning season, but it was full of newspapers now. I dug through them trying to find the one I'd read at the hospital. The paper I was looking for was all the way at the bottom of the stack. I spotted the headline: "Family of Ex–NFL Player Harassed after Moving to Briar's Cove."

This time I read the whole story. I hoped there might be something in it that would help me figure out what to do about Uncle Bix.

I found it: "The officer in charge of the case, Lieutenant Ed Turner, said a full investigation is under way. 'This behavior violates all our standards of decency,' he said. 'Besides being a crime. We will find and arrest the perpetrators.'"

I put the newspaper back in the bin and returned to the kitchen for a pencil and paper. The line I wrote to myself said, "Lieutenant Ed Turner—officer in charge."

I heard Aunt Hattie coughing, and stuffed the paper into my pocket. As I walked into her room I wondered how things could change so fast. How could she seem so healthy in the morning and look so near death tonight? I put the oxygen mask over her mouth. She was groggy and couldn't seem to keep her eyes open, but she was strong enough to pat me on the arm and smile.

Just as she stopped coughing and began breathing easier, I heard the front door open. Uncle Bix came into the room. He looked down at Aunt Hattie. He was sweating. He looked nervous and anxious about something.

"What's wrong?" I asked him.

"Nothing," he said. "I'm just concerned about your aunt, that's all."

In the seven weeks I'd been with my aunt and uncle I'd learned to recognize when Uncle Bix was upset over Aunt Hattie just by looking into his face. This wasn't one of those times. Something else was troubling him, something that had to do with the sportmen's meeting at the old church.

~ part three ~

Fires

~ fifteen ~

It was almost the end of August. Uncle Bix's worry about the changing weather deepened. Another summer storm came in, and this one lasted three days.

We weren't able to do much on the boat besides plan what we'd do after the bad weather passed. I could tell Uncle Bix didn't like being cooped up. He was in a foul mood most of the time, and had started yelling at me for no reason.

Aunt Hattie grew worse. She never got out of bed. Uncle Bix made her meals and took them to her, sitting by her until she ate what she could, which wasn't much.

One morning, Uncle Bix came out of her room and said Aunt Hattie wanted to see me. "Don't you wear her out, now," he said, as if he were the only one who cared about her.

She was sitting up with a pillow behind her back. "Uncle Bix said you wanted to talk with me," I said.

She nodded but was silent, saving her strength. She patted the edge of the mattress, letting me know she wanted me to sit there. I sat next to her. Her leg touched my side.

"How's the boat coming?" she asked. This was the first time I'd heard her talk in a couple days. Her voice had changed. It was weak and scratchy sounding. She struggled to push out words.

"Good, except this storm has slowed us down," I said.

"Stick with it," she said.

"We will."

"Good."

She turned away and gazed out the window, staring at the rainy, windy day as if her thoughts could bring back the sun. Then she looked at me again. Tears welled up in her eyes. "Strength," she said. She made a clinched fist. "Keep strong."

"I will."

Now I was the one looking out at the storm and trying to think it away. I wanted to think lots of things away, the storm, Aunt Hattie's cancer, the meetings Uncle Bix went to at the old church, Earl and Gus Hanks, my father's hatred of his brother, and the possibility that Uncle Bix might be getting into trouble again.

I turned back to Aunt Hattie. She knocked her knuckles against the little dresser next to the bed. "Pull out that drawer," she said.

I slowly opened the drawer and looked into it. On top of some papers was a picture.

"Go ahead. Look at it," she said.

I held the picture before my eyes. It was one of Uncle Bix and my father. Uncle Bix looked like he was in his early twenties. My dad was maybe nine or ten. Uncle Bix had his arm around him. The two were standing in the driveway of my grandparents' house. They were in front of some sort of weird looking vehicle, half car, half boat. Both of them were smiling.

"Your father and uncle built that thing together. They called it The Amphibious. They made it out of junk," she said. "It was some weird sort of contraption that you could drive on both land and sea."

She watched my face as I studied the photo, anxious to know what sort of effect it was having on me. "It wasn't always like it is now," she said. "Things between them, I mean."

"Yeah," I said.

All the talk was wearing Aunt Hattie out. Uncle Bix would be angry with me if he thought I was to blame. I stood up and patted her shoulder. "You rest now," I said. I started to put the photo back in the drawer. She stopped me. "No," she murmured. "You keep it."

"Okay," I said. I slipped the picture into my jeans pocket, the same one that held the note with the detective's name on it.

I looked into her eyes just before she closed them. "Remember—strength, Aunt Hattie. Be strong," I said. But I don't know if she heard me.

The storm blew over that night. Uncle Bix stood on the porch and watched as the clouds drifted across the sky and the stars came out. The clearing night lifted his mood.

He called me out to be with him. "It's over," he said, looking skyward, smiling. "So tomorrow we work hard all day."

"Good," I said. "I'm ready."

We stayed on the porch, Uncle Bix keeping his ear tilted toward the bedroom window in case Aunt Hattie needed him.

The storm had cleansed everything. The bay, the trees, the beach all looked like new, even under the shadowy light of the night sky. I liked the pure stillness left by the wind and rain. Then, suddenly, it was all torn apart by the awful sound of sirens. I saw flames rise on the far shore. A building was on fire. Fire trucks, their red lights twirling and their horns blaring, surrounded it. Hoses sprayed water on the burning structure. Uncle Bix stared at the fire. "Just a small outbuilding," he said. "Some kids probably playing with matches."

"Who does it belong to?" I asked.

He didn't answer. He turned and went back inside to be with Aunt Hattie. I could see his silhouette through the window. He leaned over the bed and kissed Aunt Hattie on the cheek. I turned away to look at the fire. It was out now, but smoke still trailed into the sky.

~ sixteen ~

The next morning I went to the end of the old dock. I scanned the north shore of the bay, searching for the remains of the burned building. The flames and sirens had made it easy to see at night, but in the daylight it was hidden in the distance. Before I could find it, Uncle Bix called out to me from the bow of Prometheus. "I need some help over here," he said.

I went to him. He was peering into Prometheus's stripped motor. He'd been squatting like a baseball catcher. When he saw me and slowly stood up, he had to catch himself from falling over. "These knees are going," he said. He wiggled one leg and then the other as if he were trying to jiggle out change that had escaped through a hole in his pocket.

"I need you to go into the shop and get me that big Crescent wrench that's hanging up just next to my lathe," he said. "Got to turn the shaft on this thing."

I nodded and marched off to the shop. Just as I was going in, the stranger in the white car drove up. He parked in front of the cabin and waited there for Uncle Bix. I stood in the doorway of the shop and watched Uncle Bix walk over to greet him. Then Uncle Bix looked at me and said, "Get that wrench and take it to the boat. Wait there for me. I'll just be a minute."

He stared at me as a way of demanding I mind my own business and do what I was told.

"Right," I said. I went into the shop but hid behind the door and watched the stranger get out of his car. I could tell he was angry. His face was red, and he shook his head back and forth as he scolded Uncle Bix under his breath, thinking I was still close enough to hear him. Then he looked around the cabin as if making sure they were alone. Raising his voice he said, "Let's go inside."

I went over to Uncle Bix's lathe and saw the big Crescent wrench hanging just where he'd said it would be. It was high on the wall, so I climbed onto the lathe to reach it. After grabbing the wrench, I looked down and noticed a newspaper on Uncle Bix's workbench. The paper was still coiled up with a rubber band. I climbed down and picked it up. It was today's edition. Aunt Hattie and Uncle Bix had the paper delivered every morning. Usually Uncle Bix picked it up at the line of mailboxes at the end of the road. Today he'd taken the paper into his shop where nobody would find it. When I read the news, I knew why.

Arsonists Send Message of Hate

Last night, arsonists set fire to a storage shed at the home of Sammy Dixon, a former offensive lineman for the Seahawks. Mr. Dixon had complained of other incidents of harassment prior to last night's fire. He . . .

I stopped reading when I thought I heard someone walking around outside. I folded the paper back up and returned it to the workbench. As I peeked around the door I saw Earl Hanks sneaking along the edge of the cabin, then standing on tiptoes to look in through the front window. I still held the Crescent wrench. He was already afraid of me, and with a weapon in my hand, he'd be sure to run off like a scared cat.

"Hey. What are you doing?" I shouted.

I stood in the open and held the wrench up so Earl could see it. He turned around, clinched his fists, and walked toward me. He wasn't afraid. He didn't care about the wrench. This time he was going to fight me.

"Who's the visitor?" he said. He gestured at the car.

"None of your business," I said. *If you stand up to a bully . . .*

He kept coming, and we walked toward each other. Just then Uncle Bix came out of the house and stood on the porch steps.

"What do you want?" Uncle Bix yelled at Earl.

Earl stopped and turned to look at Uncle Bix. "I was just about to beat up your nephew," Earl said.

My uncle chuckled. "Yeah, well, I doubt you could do that," he said. Earl's face reddened. He stuck out his jaw.

"You have company, I see," Earl said. He nodded toward the car.

"Get off my property or I'll call the cops," Uncle Bix said.

"Maybe the cops are already here," Earl said. He took a cigarette out of his shirt pocket, stuck it between his lips, and lit it.

"You heard my uncle," I said. "Leave. Now."

I approached him again. He watched my feet, then stared at the Crescent wrench. He knew I wasn't bluffing.

He exhaled some cigarette smoke through his nostrils, then turned and walked away.

"Here's your wrench," I said to Uncle Bix as he watched Earl disappear up the road.

"Good," he said. "Put it in the boat and wait there for me. I'll be out in a minute."

I climbed into Prometheus and put the wrench next to the motor. Somehow, over the course of the morning, my uncle had managed to put the Mercruiser 350 almost completely back together. Most of the parts that had been strewn all over the deck were now assembled. Prometheus's engine was almost ready to be fired up.

I leaned against the boat's port rail and examined her hull. The gash near the bow could be fixed, I thought, but there was no telling how much of her other wood was dry-rotted and would have to be replaced. And there was the '63 Chris Craft in the woods, just waiting to receive Prometheus's motor, like a person with a bad heart getting the good heart of someone who's died. But when would it happen? And why had Uncle Bix left the old motor inside Prometheus, as if the boat were still living?

Finally, Uncle Bix's visitor came out of the cabin. His face was stern and he kept his eyes on the ground. Whatever he and Uncle Bix had talked about, it was serious business. He drove away faster than he'd driven in.

Uncle Bix came right out to the boat and started working on the motor. I could tell he didn't want to talk. His mind was on Prometheus again. "Tonight we try to start her," he said.

~ seventeen ~

All day long, Uncle Bix talked about Prometheus's motor. Most of the time he spoke in that foreign boat mechanic's language of his that I didn't understand. "We'll need to re-thread those header bolts, torque down that gasket, realign that pulley, test for juice in the wires . . ."

And once again he seemed to be in a hurry. I think the speed at which he worked had something to do with Aunt Hattie, and with summer ending.

She'd gotten much worse. That day, whenever I peeked in on her, she was in a deep sleep.

We didn't get a chance to try to start Prometheus's motor that afternoon. No matter how fast Uncle Bix worked, he couldn't get all the pieces together, and one thing especially upset him. He was missing a part and would have to order it from the factory.

"I hate doing that," he said. He looked down at the engine,

at the place where the part was supposed to go. Up to now, he'd been able to restore or make new anything he needed. I'd become lost in all the details. I'd reached the point where I just watched him with fascination and wonder. I realized that no one but he could really understand what he was doing.

"It's just not the same if I can't fix or build it on my own," he said. He looked right into my eyes. He wanted the words to sink in. His voice was strong with pride. He'd never really talked much about his mechanical magic, but now he wanted me to know how special his gifts were, that he did one thing better than anybody in the world. Having to order a part from the factory made him feel like just another mechanic, I decided.

The big Crescent wrench I'd gotten out of the shop was resting on Prometheus's starboard rail. Uncle Bix looked at it and laughed softly.

"Would you really have clobbered Earl with that thing?" he said.

"Depends," I replied.

"On what?"

"If he tried to hurt us or not."

He liked the answer. He patted me on the head and then scrubbed my scalp with his knuckles. Suddenly I felt closer and more at ease with my uncle than I had all summer. I felt I could say almost anything to him.

"Tell me about The Amphibious, Uncle Bix," I said.

His eyebrows shot up and he folded his arms across his chest, as if he couldn't tell whether what I'd said was an insult or a compliment.

"Well, who told you about that?"

"Aunt Hattie. She gave me a picture of you and my dad standing next to it."

"She did, did she?"

He looked off, trying to remember.

"You know I'm quite a lot older than your dad, don't you?" he said.

"Yep."

"I could almost be his father—well, maybe not."

He laughed softly after he'd done the math in his head. He was silent for a moment, then he took a deep breath. "Well, I was about twenty-three and your dad was about eight, I think. We lived in the house you live in now."

"Grandpa built it," I offered, excitedly.

"He sure did," Uncle Bix said. He looked right at me. "How do you like living in that old place?"

"It's all right. Except it gets pretty cold sometimes."

He nodded. He'd spent his own boyhood in those chilly rooms so he knew what I meant..

"So, you want to know about The Amphibious," he said. "Okay, let's see. Back then I worked at a machine shop in the city. Do you know where the sports arena is?"

"Yeah."

"Well, the shop I worked at was about three blocks from there."

"That's a rough neighborhood now," I said.

"It was a rough neighborhood then," Uncle Bix replied.

He took a deep breath and stared off at the tops of some trees. The way he seemed to contemplate what he'd just said made me wonder if the roughness of that neighborhood had anything to do with his own misdirection, if it was where he got mixed up with the wrong crowd.

"So, what about the machine shop?" I prompted.

"Yeah, well, that shop was owned and run by a friend of your grandfather's, a man named Claude Buffcaster."

I snickered at the name "I know," Uncle Bix said. He put his hand on my shoulder and we both laughed for a moment. "But that was his real name. Claude Buffcaster. We worked on all kinds of things at Claude Buffcaster's shop—boat engines, car engines, fancy metal gates for rich folks—but everything we worked with was metal."

He bobbed his head at Prometheus's motor, as if to say "Metal, like that."

"Anyway," he went on, "Mr. Buffcaster was a very kind man and let me use whatever sort of scrap we had left over from jobs. But his kindest act was letting me use all the tools in the shop on weekends—everything, the lathes, drill presses, cutting torches, welders. Everything. I built all sorts of stuff, but nothing all that impressive until your dad came up with the idea for this amphibious thing. One day, he hit me with it. 'Let's try to build something that's half boat and half car,' he said. 'Something that can live partly in the water and partly on land, like an amphibian.' Your dad thought I could build anything he could think up. And up to then I'd pretty much been able to. But this was going to be different. This was going to be a real challenge."

I could tell my uncle loved remembering the story he was telling me. Those were better times for him and my dad. I no longer really wanted to hear about The Amphibious. I wanted him to tell me why they'd grown apart, how it was that he got mixed up with the wrong group of men.

"Did my dad help you much with it?" I asked, trying feebly to steer the conversation. Uncle Bix let out a hoot of laughter.

"I'm sure your dad has many talents, Donovan," Uncle Bix said. "But he has no skill whatsoever with mechanical things."

"I know," I said.

"You do?"

"Yeah. One day he couldn't even replace the tube in my bike tire. I had to do it myself. He just messed it up—totally."

My uncle patted me on the head. "Go easy," he said. "I'd give my right arm to play music like your dad does," he said. "He still playing in a jazz band?"

"Yep," I said. "They call themselves The Jetty Cats. They play at some club on Friday nights. I think he'd like to be a full-time musician, but he can't make enough money at it. That's why he's a teacher, I guess."

Uncle Bix let out a *how about that* sort of cackle. Then he rolled his eyes.

"Things worked out so backwards," he said. "I was the one named after a jazz musician and I'm practically tone deaf. And your dad, well, he's intimidated by a screwdriver."

I laughed softly.

"Oh, well, it doesn't matter now," Uncle Bix said. "And it didn't matter then, either."

"What didn't matter?" I asked.

"That your dad couldn't do mechanical things when we worked on The Amphibious. All that mattered was that we were doing a project together, that we were sharing a dream. Besides, it didn't work anyway."

"What?"

"The Amphibious. We took it on a test drive. It did all right on land, but it sunk when we launched her into the water."

"Sank?"

"Yep. We put her in at a landing on some backwater on

the Columbia River. She stayed afloat for maybe two minutes, and then she sank right to the bottom. We had to swim to shore. She's probably still out there."

"Did you build anything else together after that?" I asked.

"Nope. I guess you could say that was the beginning of—"

He stopped abruptly.

"Of what?" I asked.

"Of my falling-out with your dad. After The Amphibious sank, I took up with some jokers I probably should have stayed away from. Your dad, even though he was so much younger than me, could see I was making a mistake. He tried to warn me. I told him to get lost, and he did. He's stayed lost ever since. My getting busted and thrown into the can just sealed things for good between me and Ray."

For the first time that summer my uncle referred to my dad by his first name, and I realized then that it wasn't really hate that separated my dad from his brother. It was something softer and more complicated, something to do with being rejected, and let down. Saying my dad's name out loud seemed to bring this same idea into perspective for Uncle Bix. All that had gone wrong between him and his brother suddenly faced him like some evil, threatening words from a letter he'd just read.

I could tell that my uncle was truly sorry for all the mistakes he'd made in his life, that he wanted to live his life over again, do things differently, make new decisions. I wanted to tell him it wasn't too late. He could stop going to those meetings with Gus Hanks. He could stop thinking of himself as better than "those folks." He could treat people, no matter how they looked, with respect, like the way he treated me and Aunt Hattie, and the way he once had treated his brother, Ray.

~ eighteen ~

Uncle Bix had found a broken-down wheelchair and had started rebuilding it. For some reason he'd hidden it inside his shop and was sneaking out there to work on it whenever we weren't working on Prometheus or he wasn't taking care of Aunt Hattie.

I first saw the wheelchair when I happened to wander into the shop and found him squatting down next to it, poking a screwdriver underneath the seat. He didn't seem to mind at all that his secret had been revealed.

"I paid fifty cents for this at a yard sale," he said. "Can you believe that?"

"Yep," I said. I was surprised my uncle had paid *anything* for it.

"She'll be as good as new once I've made a few more adjustments," he said. "She's not as nice as the one Nurse Elliot had brought up for your Aunt Hattie at the hospital," Uncle Bix said, "but she's good enough."

"Nurse Elliot?" I said.

"Right," he said. "You know, she was there when we picked up your aunt."

I'd never learned the name of the African American nurse Aunt Hattie had thanked so much the day we brought her home. And now, strangely, it was Uncle Bix who told me, who remembered.

He was in a good mood, probably because Aunt Hattie seemed a little better this morning. When I'd gone in to check on her, she was sitting up in bed. She'd smiled at me.

Uncle Bix kept poking around the seat of the wheelchair with his screwdriver. A metal piece fell off, skipping away over the shop's wooden floor. "Blast it!" he said.

I said nothing, just stared at his fingers as he retrieved the part and secured it back into place.

"This will allow your Aunt Hattie to get outside more," he said.

Once again, I felt confused about my aunt's condition. Sometimes Uncle Bix seemed to be just trying to make things better for her in her last days. Other times he really seemed to believe she was getting better, that her lung cancer would just go away, like the flu.

"I want to have this chair up and running by this afternoon," he said. He'd been squatting. He stood and rubbed his bad knee. "We're starting the motor," he said, gleefully. "And I want to bring Hattie right next to the boat when we do it."

"Today?" I asked.

"That's right—with any luck, I mean."

I sighed. I didn't feel like working on Prometheus. This was the big event, starting Prometheus's motor. I should have been thrilled, but we'd done almost nothing except work on the boat and care for Aunt Hattie since I'd been here. I wanted to do something different. I wanted to explore the peninsula—anything. Just something different.

"What's wrong?" Uncle Bix asked.

I shrugged and sighed again.

He seemed to know what I was thinking. "Look," he said. "I'll be working on this chair for a while. Why don't you do whatever you want this morning."

"Really?"

"Yeah, really."

I turned to leave. "But be back by early afternoon," he said.

I walked back to the cabin to get something to drink. I went into the kitchen and discovered a list Uncle Bix had left on the counter. "People to Notify," he'd written at the top. Seeing the list hit me like discovering an ugly scar I didn't know I had. I realized how bad things were for Aunt Hattie.

My mom and dad were on the list, and some of Aunt Hattie's sisters and brothers who lived in Ohio. The names were written in jagged letters. My uncle's hand must have been shaking when he wrote them.

I stood next to the phone, staring at the list. Then I reached into my pocket for the piece of paper with the police officer's name on it. The longer I stared at it, the more I believed this was the man who'd visited Uncle Bix. I wanted to talk to him and find out why.

I searched the kitchen for a telephone book and finally found one in the pantry. There was so much information on the Government pages that I didn't know where to start. Finally I wrote down all the phone numbers that might work. I stared at the numbers just like I'd stared at the list of people who made up Aunt Hattie's life, as if it was somebody's secret note that I'd come across by accident.

"What are you doing?"

Uncle Bix's words jolted me. It was like someone had splashed ice water on the back of my neck.

I kept my eyes on the phone book, and didn't turn to face him.

"Donovan. I asked you what you're doing," Uncle Bix said. I could hear and feel him approach. I put the notepad inside the phone book and closed it.

"I was thinking about calling my mom and dad," I said, lying stupidly.

"You need the phone directory for that?" he said. He was right behind me now. His chest almost touched my back. He leaned his face over my shoulder. I felt his breath on my ear. I could smell him, a blend of motor oil and fresh sawdust.

"Well, no," I said. "But I was just looking—"

"Don't lie, Donovan."

We stared at each other. Uncle Bix noticed the piece of paper with the detective's name on it resting on the counter. He picked it up and held it in front of my face. "And what's this about?" he asked.

His question was sharp and direct, but I got the feeling he wasn't really mad at me. Even so, I was afraid to tell him the truth.

I turned away from him and looked out the window, toward the bay.

"Do you remember the first time you took me out in the skiff, out to where Prometheus was?" I asked. He followed my gaze out the window and considered the question.

"What about it?" he said.

"Well, I remember some advice you gave me that day," I said.

He tossed the piece of paper back onto the counter. His face softened. He chuckled. "Better not tell your father that," he said.

"Tell him what?" I asked.

"That I was giving you advice."

I kept my eyes on the piece of paper as I spoke. "You told me that a person can't go back in time and do things over again. You can't 'roll back the tape' on your life, is what you told me."

"And that's the truth," he said.

He stepped back, standing away from me in the middle of the kitchen. Aunt Hattie coughed. We both stopped to listen. Uncle Bix took a deep breath and tugged at his nose.

"No, it's *not* true," I said.

"What do you mean?" he said, as he turned and faced me.

"I mean sometimes things come back into your life again, things like the ones that happened before. You get another try at them. It's like you get another chance to—"

"Listen, Donovan." He spoke very softly now. "That cop, the one on your piece of paper there." He nodded toward the counter. "I know who he is, and I know what he is doing."

He stared at me like he'd never stared at me before. It was as if he was telling me that, no matter what I was up to, he was one step ahead of me, that whatever I was about to do, it didn't really matter, because he'd already started something he was determined to finish.

"So," he said. His voice rose again. "I came into this house to check on your Aunt Hattie, and that's what I'm going to do. Then I'm going out to my shop to work some more on her wheelchair. All right?"

"Yeah," I said. "All right."

He left. I returned the telephone book to the pantry. I picked up the piece of paper with the detective's name on it and folded it up into a tiny wad. I put it back in my pocket.

Then I took off.

I had a sour feeling about not having been more honest and forceful with Uncle Bix. Trying to make up for it, I sprinted to the old dock and decided to try walking on it with my eyes closed. Had I mastered it enough to know where the gaps were without seeing them? Could I just feel my way, without falling?

I stopped after just a few steps. The feat was impossible. I thought about what Aunt Hattie had said about making the right choices in life. Maybe stopping was the right choice. A few more steps and I would have fallen right through.

I left the dock and walked along the beach awhile. Then I went up the peninsula road to the abandoned church where Gus Hanks and Uncle Bix had their "sportsmen" meetings. I wanted to see what the old church looked like in the light of day.

It was rundown and dirty inside. There were empty beer cans and cigarette butts all over the floor and the pews. The mud nests of swallows filled the rafters. The birds dove at me, chased me out of the place, swooping down at my head until I got about halfway up the grassy hill in the nearby cemetery. I stood there and watched the swallows retreat into the cold shadows of the church.

Just then a wind came up. It swirled through my hair,

which had begun to grow back, unnoticed by Uncle Bix. It was almost as long as it was on the day I arrived here. I clawed through it, feeling good about having enough for the wind to toss about.

The wind came up again and this time it seemed colder. I looked off in the distance. Aunt Hattie and Uncle Bix's cabin was just beyond the rooftop of the abandoned church. A stream of smoke rose from the woods behind it.

I ran as fast as I could through the cemetery. I fell once and rolled over some graves, but I didn't care.

By the time I reached the road, I heard sirens approaching. In a few seconds, fire trucks were coming up behind me. I had to hurry out of their way so they could pass by me. The sirens hurt my ears.

Finally, I was close enough to see the flames. The '63 Chris Craft, the boat in the woods, was burning.

The fire trucks busted through the forest to reach it. Uncle Bix threw buckets of water on her, but it did no good. The firemen knew they couldn't save the boat, so they tried to prevent the fire from spreading into the trees.

I ran to Uncle Bix. I embraced him as he watched his dream go up in smoke. We held each other until the fire was out. Then Uncle Bix pulled away from me and walked over to the burned up Chris Craft, now just a smoldering pile of wood. He put his arms out as if he were trying to fly. He looked up and shook his fist. "I can't fix this. I just can't," he said, to someone or something bigger than himself. I hoped whoever he was talking to was listening.

~ nineteen ~

Some people think good and bad things happen in flurries, that a string of misfortunes will be followed by a chain of positive events. I don't know if I believe this or not. Maybe I haven't lived long enough to test the theory. But there was no doubt that me and Uncle Bix were in one of those times when misfortune is king.

The police came to investigate the fire. They couldn't find any natural causes for it, and suspected arson. I heard Uncle Bix's answer when they asked him if he knew why anybody might want to set fire to the Chris Craft. "No. I do not," he said, but I don't know if they believed him.

The policeman in the white car started coming by again. He and Uncle Bix spent a lot of time alone. They'd go into Uncle Bix's shop and lock the door. Uncle Bix would turn on an old fan, one he'd found in a dumpster and rebuilt, to drown out their conversation. Once, I climbed a tree— the same one I'd hidden behind when I'd looked into the detective's car—to peer into one of the shop's upper windows. I could see Uncle Bix and the detective standing next to Uncle Bix's big lathe. Both men were leaning against it, looking at each other, talking, but that was all.

As I started to get down from that tree Uncle Bix and the detective stopped talking and began leaving the shop. My shirt caught on a branch, and all I could do was stay still and watch the two men below, hoping they wouldn't look up and see me. They didn't. They both kept their eyes fixed on the ground, almost as if they were walking down a scary trail.

After the detective drove off and Uncle Bix went into the cabin, I untangled my shirt and slid down the trunk. As I brushed off my pants. I felt a wad of paper in one of my pockets. It was the note with the detective's name on it, but going through the laundry had reduced it to a soft pulpy mass. The name had been washed away.

Worst of all, there was Aunt Hattie. The day after the fire, I had to call 911 because her breathing was so weak, and she was so white. One of the ambulance attendants gave her a shot and then stood talking with Uncle Bix, shaking his head back and forth the whole time. He patted Uncle Bix on the back, as if Aunt Hattie had already died and he wanted to show his sympathy.

Nothing good happened. The wheelchair Uncle Bix had fixed up never made it out of the shop. We didn't work on Prometheus's motor. Uncle Bix spent almost all his time in the bedroom with Aunt Hattie.

Sometimes I went out to Prometheus and thought about working on the motor myself. Even though Uncle Bix had taught me a lot over the last couple months, I had no idea where to begin.

I spent a lot of time at the end of the old dock just thinking about things, all kinds of things. Why did Aunt Hattie get lung cancer? Why was Earl Hanks so mean? Was it his fault, or somebody else's?

I took walks along the beach, letting my mind wrap around the questions, thinking that maybe, when I was older, I'd be able to unravel them. One day, I saw a bald eagle. I sat on top of a rock near the surf and watched the eagle fish. I saw it swoop down and pull a Dolly Varden trout from a shallow cove.

The day I saw the eagle was the day Aunt Hattie died.

It was late in the afternoon when I came back to the cabin. Uncle Bix sat on the steps. He was stiff as a statue and stared at me with unblinking eyes as I approached. I'd never seen him look like this before. As if he were in a trance, he watched me come toward him. I wondered if he was really seeing me, or if I just happened to be in his line of sight. His expression changed as I came closer. He moved like a human being again, using the back of his hand to wipe away the stream of tears rolling down his face. I stopped.

I knew.

He lowered his head when I reached him. He couldn't look at me. "She's gone," he said.

At first, I thought only about the words he'd used. "She's gone"—as if Aunt Hattie had just taken a trip to the grocery store and would be back later. I realized it was a way for people to get around the power of death. Aunt Hattie had just started a journey, that's all. Someday we'd all see her again.

I put my hand on Uncle Bix's shoulder. I couldn't think

of anything to say. All I could do was touch him. He kept his head down. I could hear him crying. He stopped as he sensed I was leaving him to go inside. "Wait," he said.

"No," I replied.

I went into the bedroom to look at Aunt Hattie. Uncle Bix let me go. He understood. It was something I needed to do, and he wouldn't be able to stop me.

She lay with her hands folded over her chest. Her oxygen tank stood next to her. The tubes were all mangled and the mask was torn apart. I knew Uncle Bix had ripped into it just after Aunt Hattie took her last breath. Instead of fixing something, he wanted to break it into pieces that could never be put back together.

In some ways, she seemed alive, sleeping a dreamless sleep. For so long now, I'd seen her this way, but it was't the way I'd remember her. What I'd remember is the day we went to see Uncle Bix at Steilacoom, how she stood on the deck of the prison boat smoking that pipe.

"I promise to make the right choices in life," I whispered to her. I thought I saw her smile and nod, but it was just my imagination. It was what I wanted to see.

I went back outside. Uncle Bix had left the porch. He was on the old dock. I watched him climb into the skiff.

"Wait," I called. But he didn't hear me. He didn't want to hear me.

I sat on the porch steps and watched Uncle Bix take off in the skiff. For an instant I wondered if he might do something crazy, like go as far out to sea as he could and then jump in and commit suicide. What would I do if his little boat disappeared into the setting sun? In a couple of hours it would be dark. How long should I wait for him to return?

But he didn't go far. He started straight out, then stopped in the middle of the bay. He pointed his boat to the place just off the peninsula with the spruce trees, the place where Prometheus had once rested at the bottom of the sea. When he'd reached the spot and turned off his motor, he looked back at me and waved. I waved back. I didn't know what he was doing out there. Maybe he didn't know either.

He sat still in the boat. He became a statue again, stiff and lifeless, like a sail mast shaped into the figure of a man. I realized my uncle wanted to be alone on the water. It was the place he'd chosen to grieve.

I left the porch and went into his shop where I could be surrounded by all the things he'd brought back to life. I didn't worry about him. I knew, when he was finished out there, he would return.

~ twenty ~

My father once told me there would be certain things I'd have to do in life to prove I was really a man. He never said what those things might be. He'd just told me I'd know them when I saw them. I imagined they'd be things like leading an army into battle, making the football team, or winning first place in an arm wrestling contest. But I was wrong.

That night, on the day Aunt Hattie died, I faced one of those things. My dad was right. I knew it when I saw it, when I felt it.

After Uncle Bix returned to the cabin, he handed me the People to Notify list. "I want you to make some calls for me," he said. His voice was matter-of-fact. Being alone on the water had given him strength. He talked to me as if I were working with him on the boat motor.

"I want you to call the people on this list and tell them that your Aunt Hattie has passed away. Most of them are her friends, her family. Most of them never had much use for me. You tell them you're her nephew. You tell them she's passed away. You tell them we'll let them know in a day or two about the funeral and all that. You tell them . . ."

He turned away sharply, but stopped just before he left the kitchen. Without looking at me, he said, "I'll see to the other things. But you call those people, 'cause they've got no use for me."

My mom and dad were first on the list. Gus Hanks had been last, but his name had been crossed out.

Between my parents' and Gus Hanks's names were the names of people I didn't know. They had to be Aunt Hattie's friends and relatives. A number of them had the same last name, "Dickins." That must have been Aunt Hattie's name before she married uncle Bix, I thought. *Hattie Dickins, Hattie Dickins*—I whispered the name to myself for a while.

I liked the sound of it.

I decided to call the Dickins people first before I called my mom and dad. I don't know why I decided to do this. I just did.

I rehearsed my words. "Hello. My name is Donovon Sanger. I'm Hattie Sanger's nephew, and I'm calling with some very sad news. . . ."

It wasn't fair, I thought. Why hadn't *I* had time to think about Aunt Hattie's passing, to go off and grieve in my own private place like Uncle Bix had? Why did I have to do this dirty work just because people had hard feelings toward Uncle Bix, because they "had no use" for him?

But I also realized this was my challenge. I had to do something I didn't want to do. It was something that needed to be done and, at this time and in this place, I was the only one who could do it. People were depending on me.

My hands trembled as I punched in the first set of numbers. Everyone on the list must have known Aunt Hattie was about to die. No one was shocked by the news. Her older brother, a man named Benjamin, said, "I'm just relieved she isn't suffering anymore." Then his voice broke as he thanked me for letting him know. "This has to be hard for you, son," he said.

"Yeah," I said. "It is."

No one I talked to asked about Uncle Bix. They never even mentioned his name. Their grudges against him must be deep, I thought. And that wasn't right. If they only knew how much he loved Aunt Hattie. If they only knew about the way he'd cock his ear toward the cabin whenever we were out on the skiff. If they only knew about Prometheus.

Finally I had only Mom and Dad to call. I decided to check on Uncle Bix first. I could hear him crying behind the door. This was the first time I'd heard a man cry. In a way it was like Aunt Hattie's cough, that sound of a chain being dragged over rocks. But it was different, leading toward something instead of away from it.

I knocked. "Are you all right, Uncle Bix?" I said. He stopped weeping, cleared his throat, and said, "Have you finished making those calls?"

"No," I said.

He sighed.

"I need you to do that for me, son," he said. "You need to do that!"

"I know," I said. "I will."

I returned to the kitchen. I stared at the phone, then picked it up and called my parents. Dad answered. He knew something was wrong as soon as he heard my voice.

"What's the matter, Donny?" he asked. He called me Donny only when he knew I had something to say that I didn't want to say.

"It's Aunt Hattie." Then I used the same words Uncle Bix had used: "She's gone."

"When?"

"This morning."

"Put your uncle on the line."

"What?"

"Your Uncle Bix. Go get him. Put him on the phone."

I hurried to the bedroom. I knocked on the door. This time I could hear nothing.

"Uncle Bix," I said, "my dad wants to talk to you."

He waited to speak. Then his voice beat against the door. *"What?"*

"My dad wants to talk to you. He's on the phone."

I wondered how long it had been since Dad and Uncle Bix had spoken to each other. Had they ever spoken since Uncle Bix went to prison?

He opened the door and stood before me. His eyes were swollen and red. "He wants to speak to *me?*" Uncle Bix asked.

"Yeah," I answered. He looked as if I'd just told him Aunt Hattie hadn't really died, that it was all a bad dream.

"All right, then," he said. He slid past me. I stood in the hall and listened.

"Ray, is that you?" Uncle Bix said.

I peeked around the door so I could see Uncle Bix's face. He looked at his feet and stuffed one hand into the pocket of his jeans. He looked like a shy child being forced to speak up.

"Yeah," he said. I don't know what my father was saying,

but I could tell Uncle Bix appreciated his words. "Yeah," Uncle Bix said again. "He certainly is, Ray. You've raised yourself a wonderful son."

I stepped back. I didn't like hearing people talk about me. Even though I was being praised, I still didn't like it. And just then I didn't feel like a "wonderful son." In some ways, I felt like I'd let people down. I'd been sent here to help out, but Aunt Hattie had died, and Uncle Bix might be in trouble again.

"In the morning?" Uncle Bix said to my dad. "All right, then. That would be fine."

I heard Uncle Bix hang up the phone. He left the kitchen and saw me standing in the hall. He knew I'd been listening, but it didn't matter to him. In some ways I think he wanted me to hear what was being said.

"Your dad and mom are going to be here first thing in the morning. They're going to help us with things."

"Good," I said. And it was good. It was the best news I'd had in a long, long time.

~ twenty-one ~

I wanted to tell Aunt Hattie what she'd done, how she'd brought my dad and Uncle Bix back together after all their years of bitterness. Later that night, I went by myself into the woods to talk to her.

I wanted to find a clearing in the forest, so I could look up into the starry night. I don't know whether I believe in heaven or not, but if Aunt Hattie were anywhere, she'd be there.

I took the trail that led to what was left of the '63 Chris Craft. I smelled the dampened ashes and saw the vague outline of the boat on the ground. The fire hadn't destroyed it completely. Its burned image remained.

Looking toward the line of trees, I saw a stack of planks I hadn't noticed before. I walked over to the pile of wood and bent down to look closer at it. Stuck under the metal straps holding the timbers together was a cardboard sign:

"Pressure-treated Douglas fir," it said. "For fixing the old dock." It looked like Uncle Bix's writing.

I smiled as I read it. When I moved back into the clearing I sensed someone was following me. I didn't hear or see anyone, but I felt them.

The feeling grew stronger once I was in the open. I looked around for a rock or a tree branch to use as a weapon. I was more angry than afraid. This was my time to talk to Aunt Hattie, and someone was intruding.

I stood still. The moon wasn't full, but it was bright in the clear sky. I heard things scampering about, the hoot of an owl, and then the voice of a person.

"It's the wimp, out here feeling sad 'cause his aunt just croaked."

Earl Hanks stood on the edge of the meadow. He looked bigger this time. He was wearing a large jacket, his hands stuffed into the front pockets. In some ways, he looked unreal, like a shadow cast by something unseen. But there was no mistaking that belligerent voice of his.

"Or is he out here crying over the fact that his uncle is nothing but a crazy—"

"Go away," I said.

"No. I won't go away," Earl said.

Earl walked toward me. I didn't move. I was ready to fight him, though I feared he might have a weapon stuffed into his jacket. But I wasn't going to run.

"What do you want?" I said. I stared at his pockets.

"I want to get even," he said.

"For what?"

He took a few more steps, stopping when he was only

about ten feet away. Did he really have a gun or was he bluffing like before, like most bullies did? Suddenly, he turned to a sound coming out of the dark woods. It was my chance to pounce on him, but before I could do anything Earl turned and started to run. Someone rushed out of the trees and was on top of him in what seemed like an instant. Earl didn't fight back. He let the stranger throw him face down, pull his arms behind his back, and put handcuffs on him.

Two others came out of the forest. Both held flashlights and pistols. They wore police uniforms. "Just don't move," one of them said to me. He shined his light on Earl and the man on the ground. Earl's face was concealed in the grass, but I could see the face of the man who was holding him down. It was the police officer who'd been coming to visit Uncle Bix, the one with the white car. He looked up at me and asked if I was all right.

"Yeah," I said. "Who are you?"

"I'm a police officer, son," he said. "Lieutenant Ed Turner."

"But—"

"Look," he said. "This is done with. You go home now. It's over."

I nodded and turned to walk away. My heart was racing.

"Wait," the detective said. I stopped and looked over my shoulder at him. "Can you keep this a secret for a while?"

"Yeah," I said. "I can."

I didn't go home. I hid in the trees and watched as the policemen took Earl away. I didn't really understand what had just happened, but I didn't care. I'd come to this place to talk to Aunt Hattie, and that's what I was going to do.

I went back to the very spot where Earl had been wrestled to the ground. I could hear cars driving off into the distance. They were taking Earl to the police station, I thought, then maybe to Juvenile Hall. Maybe someday he would end up in Steilacoom, like his father and Uncle Bix. In some ways, I felt sorry for him. Maybe if his father had been different, he would have been different. Maybe, in some ways, it wasn't his fault.

The noise from the cars died away. I looked up at the stars. The sky seemed brighter than before, and it was quieter. It reminded me of how things were after the big storm had passed, clean and peaceful. I needed peace.

"Aunt Hattie," I said. I didn't whisper. I spoke in a full voice. "I don't know where you are right now. People have lots of different ideas about these kinds of things, you know, life after death, and all that. I just don't know. But I'm going to talk to you anyway. I hope you can hear me.

"So many things happened today, and in a strange sort of way, I think they all have something to do with you. I can't explain it, but I just feel it inside.

"My mom and dad are coming up tomorrow to help Uncle Bix. Uncle Bix and my dad actually talked tonight, and they didn't sound mad at each other. It's because of you, Aunt Hattie."

I lowered my eyes and kicked at the ground. The sadness I'd been holding inside burst out of me. I cried, but kept talking.

"And did you see what just happened here? The cops came and got Earl Hanks just before he was going to do something bad to me. They . . ."

I stopped and took some deep breaths. Suddenly I could think of nothing to say, nothing except one last question. "Can you hear me, Aunt Hattie?"

I waited a moment, then turned and started walking back to the cabin. The night was colder now. The cabin, with the soft light shining in the windows, seemed close and distant at the same time. I looked past the cabin to the sea, and to the moonlight spreading over the water, and to the shooting star falling just above where Prometheus had lain. There was Aunt Hattie, I thought.

That was her answer.

~ twenty-two ~

I was the first to get up the next morning. All summer Uncle Bix had been awake before me. Sometimes I wondered if he ever slept.

The cabin was cold. I could see my breath. Summer was ending.

I went outside to the woodpile. I'd made a lot of progress splitting those rounds during the last few weeks. Now I could enjoy the fruits of my labor, I thought, if the wood was dry enough.

I gathered some of the smaller pieces of split pine and took them into the cabin. This would be the first fire of the season in the woodstove, and I would be the one to make it.

I was good at making fires. The old house my grandpa built had a fireplace in it, and Dad had taught me when I was very young how to get flames going without smoking up the living room.

The pine was good and dry, but I needed some newspaper for starting my fire. I looked in the copper bin by the woodstove and found some. The paper on top was yesterday's edition. I gasped when I saw the headline, and the picture of Gus Hanks under it.

Undercover Operation Leads to Arrest of White Supremacist

Yesterday, police arrested Gus F. Hanks, 50, for allegedly conspiring to commit a series of hate crimes against a local African American family. Charges were brought against Mr. Hanks for arson and harassment, as well as a host of misdemeanors. Police said there would likely be more arrests.

The arrest of Hanks came after an ongoing investigation carried out by both federal and local law enforcement agencies. Recent evidence for the charges against Hanks was obtained using an unpaid informant . . .

I folded up the paper. I would save it forever, not burn it. I dug deep into the pile and found some ads from a sportsman's store, to use instead.

Once the fire was going, I sat in front of the stove, staring into the flames. I thought about how fires like this one could be good things, and others, like the one that burned the '63 Chris Craft, did nothing but hurt people.

I also wondered why Uncle Bix wasn't awake yet. It wasn't like him to stay in bed past dawn. But so much had happened to him lately, I thought, maybe it was a good time for him to change his habits if he wanted to.

The cabin warmed fast. The little stove put out more heat than I thought it would. When I went outside to stand on the porch I spotted Uncle Bix out by Prometheus. He's been out here all night, I thought, working under the soft light of a kerosene lantern. I hadn't even noticed him when I'd come out to gather the firewood. He'd pulled off the wounded planks near Prometheus's bow, exposing the inside of her hull. He'd just stuck his head inside the void, like a lion tamer poking his face between the jaws of a lion. He shined the beam of his flashlight around her ribs. I wondered what he was looking for.

As I watched him, I wanted to tell him about what had happened with Earl Hanks and the detective the night before, but I didn't. In a strange way, I sensed Uncle Bix already knew.

So I left him alone. I understood he needed to be out there by himself, working on the boat.

~ ~ ~

Uncle Bix quit working on Prometheus only after my parents arrived. I was on the porch, waiting for them. Uncle Bix let me go to them first when they drove up. Then he approached slowly, carrying a pair of pliers. He seemed to forget he was holding the tool, quickly stuffing it into his back pocket just before he reached us.

This was the first time in my life I'd seen my parents with Uncle Bix. Just after I'd hugged my mom and dad, my uncle entered our small circle. He stood tense, with his back straight, as if he was standing before a judge about to sentence him for a crime. At first, my mom and dad didn't want to look at him. They kept their eyes on me, but I tried to divert their gaze until finally they had to face my uncle.

"We are very, very sorry, Bix," my dad said. His voice was different. I didn't recognize it. "You know how much we loved Hattie," he added.

It was my mom who broke through the invisible barrier. She stepped forward and hugged my uncle. He didn't hug her back. He just stood there with his hands at his side.

"Thank you," he murmured.

Just then another car drove up. It was the police detective, Lieutenant Turner. We all turned our heads to him. I could tell that Uncle Bix wished the man hadn't arrived so abruptly, hadn't disrupted such a delicate moment.

The detective sat in his car, seeming uncomfortable under all our stares. But he soon got out and came over to us.

My parents looked at Uncle Bix and silently asked that he introduce the man. My uncle poked at the ground with his boot, then gave in.

"Detective Turner, this is my brother, Ray, and his wife, Martha."

My parents stiffened with shock and disappointment. I knew by the expression on their faces that they thought Uncle Bix was in trouble with the law again.

"We need to go, Bix," said the detective, who seemed so much gentler than the other night. "We have that appointment, remember. I know this is a bad time. But we need to do it. The sooner the better."

"Right," Uncle Bix said. Then he shifted his eyes back and forth from Detective Turner to my parents, as if he and the detective were talking in a silent language only they understood. I saw the detective nod. Then he looked right at my dad and said, "May I have a word with you, Mr. Sanger?"

"Certainly," my dad said.

My dad and Detective Turner walked to the edge of the old dock. Both looked down the row of planks and decided not to set foot on it.

Mom put her arm around me. She pulled me away from Uncle Bix as if she'd just found out he had some terrible contagious disease. "No, Mom!" I said. "It's all right. I know it is! It's all right."

She shushed me.

Uncle Bix put his head down and walked back to Prometheus.

I pressed myself against my mom as I watched the detective talk to my father. The expression on Dad's face changed as he took in the words, going from dread to pleasant surprise.

My mom loosened her grip on me, and now it felt good being so close to her. I could smell her perfume and her freshly washed clothes. "Do you know what this is about?" she whispered to me.

"Yes," I said. "I think I do."

The detective and my dad returned. Uncle Bix had been watching them out of the corner of his eye. When he saw them come over, he too approached us. As my dad got closer, I noticed he had tears forming in his eyes.

"So, are you ready, Bix?" Detective Turner said.

"Right," Uncle Bix said. Then my dad went over to his brother. He laid his hand on Uncle Bix's shoulder and said five words I never thought I'd hear him say, "I'm proud of you, brother."

Uncle Bix and Detective Turner drove off. They were gone all day.

My parents and I ate lunch and cleaned up the cabin. Then my mom drove back to Portland to pick up The Two H's at the babysitter's. Tomorrow she would return with my sisters, and all of us would attend Aunt Hattie's funeral.

After Mom left, Dad and I went out to Prometheus. Dad climbed inside of her and stared at the motor. "Let me guess," Dad said. "Your uncle totally rebuilt this?"

"Yep," I said.

"I told you. He's a genius, isn't he?"

"Yep."

I stood next to Dad inside the boat. We both just stared at that motor, not saying anything for a moment. Then Dad put his arm around my shoulder. It seemed, at that moment, that we were closer than we'd ever been.

"You know, Donovan," he said. "I want to tell you how much I appreciate what you've done here—helping your uncle, I mean."

"Sure," I said.

He took a deep breath.

"Do you know the reason that detective was here?" he asked.

"Yeah," I said.

"You do?"

"Yeah."

"You understand that your uncle put himself at risk so the detective could apprehend some pretty bad people?" Dad said.

"Yeah," I said. "I understand."

Dad put his hand on my shoulder and squeezed it.

"He's downtown right now with the detective," Dad said. "He's making a sworn statement about how he was present at meetings where a group of men, led by some thug named Hanks, had been plotting ways to drive an African American family off the Sound. These men were like a small, sick army, planning their terrible and stupid missions."

"And Uncle Bix turned them in," I said.

"That's right, Donovan. He fixed it for them."

I didn't say anything. Dad looked at me and smiled. We hugged each other. We stared at the rebuilt motor again, as if it were some magical window through which we could see all that had happened, and all the good things the future would bring.

~ twenty-three ~

The Two H's and my mom returned the next morning. Holly and Heather wore flowery dresses and straw hats. They looked like they were going to church on Easter Sunday, not to a funeral.

Uncle Bix wanted it this way. He wanted us all to dress up in bright, joyful colors for Aunt Hattie. My mom brought back suits and ties for me and my dad to wear. Uncle Bix spent almost all morning getting ready. I hardly recognized him when he finally came out of the bedroom.

He wore a well-pressed, white suit and shiny wing-tip shoes. His hair had grown some without my having noticed. It was long enough for him to part it to one side. He looked so much better this way.

Aunt Hattie's service was at a little church about ten miles away. I don't know what denomination it was. It was just a church like any other church, but it was clean, with bright stained glass, fresh white paint, lots of green grass in front, and full of friendly people.

I sat up front with Uncle Bix and the rest of my family. I was between The Two H's. They didn't make a sound. Somehow, something or someone—God, maybe—made sure they kept quiet.

The pastor was a tall, thin man with a bold and clear voice. He didn't know Aunt Hattie that well, but he talked about her as if he'd followed alongside her throughout her life. He talked about where she was born, in Toledo, Ohio, in 1938. When she was eighteen, she moved, alone, to Chicago to work in a watch factory. Then, a few years later, she went to beautician's school so she could open up her own beauty shop. "This was her dream," the pastor said.

After she got out of beautician school, she traveled, all by herself, to Washington. There was no particular reason she chose to go to Washington, except, the pastor said, she loved how green it was. And, unlike most people, she liked the rain.

"Imagine her courage," the pastor said. "Here she was, a single woman in her midtwenties, migrating all alone to the West Coast to start her own business. Imagine the strength of character," he said.

She started her beauty shop in downtown Seattle, and that's where she met Uncle Bix. He was working at a boat repair shop down on the docks. The pastor didn't say how she and Uncle Bix met. He just mentioned the year they were married, 1963, the same year the Chris Craft in the woods had been built.

Uncle Bix broke down when the pastor said these things,

but he gathered himself and walked clear-eyed with his back straight as we left the church and stood under the bright sun. The Two H's started wrestling on the green grass. Uncle Bix took pleasure in watching them, even when their play turned to fighting. They seemed to be telling him, in their own special way, that life goes on.

~ ~ ~

The African American man is gone now. I look into the hand he'd just squeezed into numbness. I use it to brush the hair out of my eyes so I can see my father and my Uncle Bix come out of the cabin and walk side by side to Prometheus. They move to the boat as if they are marching into battle.

Uncle Bix leads the way. He looks good. His back is straight and his head is up. I imagine he looks like he did on the day he was freed from prison, when Aunt Hattie was there at the gate, waiting for him.

They reach Prometheus. Uncle Bix stands next to the boat and starts waving his hands like a conductor directing a symphony. He's telling my father all about how we pulled up this small boat that was once at the bottom of the sea and restored its engine. I can't hear all of his words, only the ones he speaks just before the two of them climb aboard. "Now we try to start her," he says.

My father and his brother lean over the motor. Dad hands Uncle Bix tools while Uncle Bix works his magic.

I hear the squeal and rumble of metal, and then the even roar of a Mercruiser 350, running perfectly.

I leave the old dock and approach Uncle Bix and my

father. They see me coming. Uncle Bix shuts down the motor so we can talk.

"Guess what?" he says.

"What?" I reply.

"Well, I think we can use her—Prometheus, I mean."

I think back to the way Uncle Bix had inspected Prometheus's hull, searching inside her with his flashlight like a miner looking for gold.

"I've checked her out," he goes on. He has that boylike tone in his voice again. "Her dry rot's not that bad. If we replace some wood, seal her up and paint her, we can leave the motor right where she is."

"We?" I ask. "I'm going home, Uncle Bix."

My words jolt him a little. Then he and my dad look at each other. They both smile big at the same time, as if they know something I don't know and are taking pleasure in the secret. "Well, there's next summer," Uncle Bix says. "I'll be working on other people's boats over the winter. I'll just let Prometheus sit awhile. You can come back next June. You come back and we'll finish this project we started. Maybe we'll even repair that dangerous old dock. Someday a man's going to hurt himself on that thing."

He looks at my dad again. They keep sharing the big smile. "Is that all right with you, Ray?" Uncle Bix says.

"It certainly is, Bix," Dad says. Then Dad scrubs my head with his knuckles, just as Uncle Bix had done when I'd first come here to visit, to help. "That all right with you, son?"

"Yeah," I say. "It's all right with me."

I turn away from my uncle and father and gaze out past the place I'd been on the old dock. There are flocks of seabirds above the water. They look like clouds of ash shifting about as one thing in the sky. I watch the birds until they disappear into the horizon. Then I think gladly about what's ahead of me and my family. I see myself in the heart of another summer on Puget Sound. Uncle Bix, me, and my dad are taking a ride in Prometheus, bucking waves in the open ocean, testing the boat's power and seaworthiness. From the bow of the boat I look back to shore and see Aunt Hattie sitting on the porch of the cabin. She's in her rocking chair, but now she's rocking. She's smiling and her hair's being pushed back by the wind, as if she's riding with us, pointing the way with her wisdom, and strength.

While writing fiction, **John Thomson** has also worked as a wildlife biologist and conservationist for over twenty years. He lives in Penn Valley, California, with his wife, Carolee, and his teenage daughters, Claire and Liv. *A Small Boat at the Bottom of the Sea* is his first novel.

If you enjoyed this book, you'll also want to read
these other Milkweed novels.

To order books or for more information,
contact Milkweed at (800) 520-6455
or visit our Web site (www.milkweed.org).

The $66 Summer
John Armistead

MILKWEED PRIZE FOR CHILDREN'S LITERATURE
NEW YORK PUBLIC LIBRARY BEST BOOKS OF THE YEAR: "BOOKS FOR
THE TEEN AGE"

A story of interracial friendships in the segregation-
era South.

The Return of Gabriel
John Armistead

A story of Freedom Summer.

The Ocean Within
V. M. Caldwell

MILKWEED PRIZE FOR CHILDREN'S LITERATURE

Focuses on an older child adopted into a large,
extended family.

Tides
V. M. Caldwell

The sequel to *The Ocean Within,* this book deals with
the troubles of older siblings.

Alligator Crossing
Marjory Stoneman Douglas

Features the wildlife of the Everglades just before it was declared a national park.

Perfect
Natasha Friend

MILKWEED PRIZE FOR CHILDREN'S LITERATURE

A thirteen-year-old girl struggles with bulimia after her father dies.

Parents Wanted
George Harrar

MILKWEED PRIZE FOR CHILDREN'S LITERATURE

Focuses on the adoption of a boy with ADD.

The Trouble with Jeremy Chance
George Harrar

BANK STREET COLLEGE BEST CHILDREN'S BOOKS OF THE YEAR

Father-son conflict during the final days of World War I.

No Place
Kay Haugaard

Based on a true story of Latino youth who create an inner-city park.

The Monkey Thief
Aileen Kilgore Henderson

NEW YORK PUBLIC LIBRARY BEST BOOKS OF THE YEAR: "BOOKS FOR THE TEEN AGE"

A twelve-year-old boy is sent to live with his uncle in a Costa Rican rain forest.

Hard Times for Jake Smith
Aileen Kilgore Henderson

A girl searches for her family in the Depression-era South.

The Summer of the Bonepile Monster
Aileen Kilgore Henderson

MILKWEED PRIZE FOR CHILDREN'S LITERATURE

A brother and sister spend the summer with their great-grandmother in the South.

Treasure of Panther Peak
Aileen Kilgore Henderson

NEW YORK PUBLIC LIBRARY BEST BOOKS OF THE YEAR: "BOOKS FOR THE TEEN AGE"

A twelve-year-old girl adjusts to her new life in Big Bend National Park.

I Am Lavina Cumming
Susan Lowell

MOUNTAINS & PLAINS BOOKSELLERS ASSOCIATION AWARD

This lively story culminates with the 1906 San Francisco earthquake.

The Boy with Paper Wings
Susan Lowell

This story about a feverish boy's imagined battles includes paper-folding instructions.

The Secret of the Ruby Ring
Yvonne MacGrory

A blend of time travel and historical fiction set in 1885 Ireland.

Emma and the Ruby Ring
Yvonne MacGrory

A tale of time travel to nineteenth-century Ireland.

A Bride for Anna's Papa
Isabel R. Marvin

MILKWEED PRIZE FOR CHILDREN'S LITERATURE

A vivid story of the courage it takes to live on Minnesota's iron range in the early 1900s.

Minnie
Annie M. G. Schmidt

A cat turns into a woman and helps a hapless newspaperman.

The Dog with Golden Eyes
Frances Wilbur

MILKWEED PRIZE FOR CHILDREN'S LITERATURE

A young girl's dream of owning a dog comes true, but it may be more than she's bargained for.

Behind the Bedroom Wall
Laura E. Williams

MILKWEED PRIZE FOR CHILDREN'S LITERATURE
JANE ADDAMS PEACE AWARD HONOR BOOK

Tells a story of the Holocaust through the eyes of a young girl.

The Spider's Web
Laura E. Williams

A young girl in a neo-Nazi group sets off a chain of events when she's befriended by an old German woman.

Milkweed Editions

Founded in 1979, Milkweed Editions is the largest independent, nonprofit literary publisher in the United States. Milkweed publishes with the intention of making a humane impact on society, in the belief that good writing can transform the human heart and spirit. Within this mission, Milkweed publishes in five areas: fiction, nonfiction, poetry, children's literature for middle-grade readers, and the World As Home—books about our relationship with the natural world.

Join Us

Milkweed depends on the generosity of foundations and individuals like you, in addition to the sales of its books. In an increasingly consolidated and bottom-line-driven publishing world, your support allows us to select and publish books on the basis of their literary quality and the depth of their message. Please visit our Web site (www.milkweed.org) or contact us at (800) 520-6455 to learn more about our donor program.

Interior design by Rachel Holscher.
Typeset in Perpetua 12.5/15
by Stanton Publication Services, Inc.
Printed on acid-free 55# Sebago 2000 Antique paper
by Maple-Vail Book Manufacturing.